HOW IT HAPPENS

JEAN ALICIA ELSTER

WAYNE STATE UNIVERSITY PRESS
DETROIT

ISBN: 978-0-8143-4869-7 (paperback); ISBN: 978-0-8143-4870-3 (e-book)

Library of Congress Control Number: 2021934632

Cover vector art © Shutterstock.
Cover design by Chelsea Hunter.

Wayne State University Press rests on Waawiyaataanong, also referred to as Detroit, the ancestral and contemporary homeland of the Three Fires Confederacy. These sovereign lands were granted by the Ojibwe, Odawa, Potawatomi, and Wyandot Nations, in 1807, through the Treaty of Detroit. Wayne State University Press affirms Indigenous sovereignty and honors all tribes with a connection to Detroit. With our Native neighbors, the press works to advance educational equity and promote a better future for the earth and all people.

Wayne State University Press
Leonard N. Simons Building
4809 Woodward Avenue
Detroit, Michigan 48201-1309

Visit us online at wsupress.wayne.edu

To my ancestors, Addie Jackson and Tom Martin—
Because of you, I am

ACKNOWLEDGMENTS

Many people have contributed to my ability to write this book: the writer's craft, though it is a solitary endeavor, is not pursued alone. While I will not try to list them all, I, in particular, offer my utmost gratitude to the following people—

To Tim Pulley, the genealogy department supervisor at Clarksville/Montgomery County Public Library in Tennessee, who unearthed and shared a treasure trove of documents and information on the Jackson and Henry/Martin family histories during my visit in the year 2000;

To the Ragdale Foundation, Lake Forest, Illinois, for that first writer's residency, where I wrote the initial draft of the opening chapters of this book;

To my Wayne State University Press editors, Kathy Wildfong and Annie Martin, for warmly welcoming book 3 of the Ford family trilogy and for pushing me out of my comfort zone to complete the book they both knew I could write;

To my dear son, Isaac Elster, editor extraordinaire, whose deep read of chapter 1 of this book helped to set the remaining chapters on the right course;

To my cousin, Darryl Ford Williams (daughter of Douglas

Ford Jr.), for unwittingly prodding me along as I worked to complete this book;

To my deceased grandmother, Maber Jackson Ford, for sharing her story with me, over and over, until it became a part of my story;

To my deceased mother, Jean Ford Fuqua, and my aunt, Maber Ford Hill, for wanting me to know what they remember;

To my sister, Gwynn Fuqua, for helping me fit the pieces together;

But, most of all, to my husband Bill, for being the light in this writer's life and living proof that "the greatest of these is love."

PROLOGUE

"Grandma, are you white?"

It's one of my earliest memories as a toddler: standing in my grandparents' kitchen, looking up at my grandmother's face as she sat at the kitchen table and asking her if she's white. I had no idea what I was asking or what that term "white" meant when it was applied to another person. Obviously, I knew that her skin was very much lighter—brighter, my grandmother would say—than my brown skin. And I had also obviously heard that word bandied about as adults talked around me. But at that age I had no concept of race or ethnic heritage. I just knew she looked different from the other family members that I interacted with.

I also did not know this: her color represented a vivid reminder of the history of racial relationships in the American South as it relates to the sexual interactions between blacks and whites and the resulting offspring that did often come from those unions. That history is fraught with complexities.

A response to those relationships was the term "miscegenation," which was created in the South in 1863 within the context of American racism and slavery. The *Merriam Webster*

Dictionary defines miscegenation as "a mixture of races especially: marriage, cohabitation, or sexual intercourse between a white person and a member of another race." It was a dominant term in many of the "race laws" that proliferated throughout much of the country. Those laws forbade black people from partaking in many aspects of American life but, in particular, banned intimate relationships between whites and people of color. The focus, if not in explicit words then at least in intent, was especially upon those relationships between black men and white women.

When those banned intimate relationships in the "race laws" occurred between white men and black women, the dynamic was altered considerably. Because beginning with the time of black enslavement in America when blacks were considered the owners' chattel, or human property, white men—even those who did not own enslaved women—could force a black woman to submit to an intimate relationship without fear of ever facing the consequences of having broken one of those "race laws."

Now, any sexual encounter that occurs without the consent of one of the parties or that occurs after a party says, "No," is rape. Period. And even more compelling are those instances where a party is afraid to say, "No," or when they know that saying no is not an option. It is still rape, and the situation and its consequences become all the more chilling.

This book begins in the post–Reconstruction era of American history, in the year my grandmother was born in 1890 in Clarksville, Tennessee. It incorporates many of the snippets of family and social history that my grandmother shared with me while I was a young child and, later, while growing up. As a child, I did not know the meaning of or the social and familial impact of many of the seemingly innocuous tales she shared with me. But what became clear to me as I reached adulthood and began to truly absorb much of what she had told me, was that even though those post–Reconstruction "race laws" have, since the 1960s, been repealed or struck down by judicial venues all the way up to the United States Supreme Court, the effects of the race-based societal and sexual double standards and injustices that emanated from those laws are still an ingrained part of our American culture. The results will continue to be felt in this country for generations to come.

1

1890

BOARDINGHOUSE

Addie Jackson felt the spasm coming beneath her belly as she made her way out of Tom Mitchell's room with his grandmother's quilt wrapped loosely around her. It was obvious to anyone who looked at the way she carried herself that the baby was due any day now. She leaned toward the railing along the second-floor hallway, then let the quilt fall as she turned, fell forward, and grabbed the rail with both hands, grabbed it with all of her might. She crouched down in a squat as the spasm took hold of her. She tried to hold in the howl as the pain welled up inside, but it was no use. She could not keep silent.

She closed her eyes and screamed, "Aaarrgh!" She held the railing so tightly she felt it move, as if it might give way.

"Addie? Addie, hold on now, girl!" Addie looked down through the railing posts. It was Tom, standing in the foyer just beneath the railing. "Good Lord," she heard him whisper, "don't let that child be born here at Mrs. Beatty's place." She could see how he strained to see her up beyond the foot of the railing. "Addie," he said in full voice, "listen to me now. I'll be right there. I'm still looking for Mrs. Beatty . . ."

Addie could hear the panic in his voice. Then she heard his footsteps as he quickly strode to the back of the house.

"Wait—come back here!" she called out to Tom Mitchell. Then she caught her breath. "Oh my God, oh my God," she panted. "Oooohhhh!" she moaned. Her hands were on the floor now as she braced herself and scooted across the floor, pushing herself away from the railing, across the worn hallway rug—dragging the quilt with her—and propped herself against the wall. As she leaned back, she looked through the posts, past the foyer, and to the front door. It was late afternoon, and the other boarders would be walking through that door soon, walking through the foyer and then into the parlor or upstairs to their rooms.

For now, Addie was alone upstairs. Yet she could hear in her head the voice of the midwife—when she was birthing Patsy, her first child—telling her, "Don't push now. It's not time to push just yet . . ."

But it was no use—she could not help herself. She pushed, and she pushed hard. And then it was gone: the spasm stopped. She breathed deeply, in and out, and then murmured, "Thank you, dear God. Thank you, Jesus."

Other women Addie talked to—neighbors or women around church—said the second birthing is always easier. Addie still remembered birthing Patsy, going on two years ago, and the rough time she had of it. But the spasms for this second baby were worse, much worse. She breathed deeply and tilted her head back against the wall.

"Tom Mitchell," Addie said his name quietly and closed her eyes. "Another baby, Tom Mitchell."

She wanted him there by her side to comfort her. She wanted to hear him say her name. "My Addie," he would greet her when he entered his room and saw her sitting by the open window. "My Addie," he would whisper later as she sat next to him on the settee, her head resting against his shoulder.

Addie jumped in place. She was startled by Mrs. Beatty's shrill tone of voice, a tone Addie had not heard her use before when talking to a white man, "Why Mr. Mitchell, this has never happened in my boardinghouse . . ." Then she heard Tom say, she could not quite make out what, but something like, "horse and buggy . . . boy." The sound of their voices trailed off.

She felt another spasm coming on and she rubbed her belly hard.

How'd it get to this?

Then she let out a long sigh because she knew full well how it happened.

When I started working for Mrs. Beatty . . . that's when everything changed . . .

Addie recalled the years that led up to her working for Mrs. Beatty. Way back when—as the youngest child of Gabe and Laura Scott—she worked the tobacco patch at the Shelby farm with her parents, brothers, and sisters. The children went to school when they could, whenever there was a teacher for the colored school. But teachers came and went and, in between, the Scott children worked the farm. Then Laura Scott took in laundry from some of the white families around Clarksville to bring in extra money, and Addie was the only one of the sisters to help the mother as she ironed. The work was hot and hard. Addie lugged the heavy irons, hot off the wood-burning stove in the kitchen, to her mother as she worked on the board laid out on the kitchen table. Addie carried pots of hot water from the stove out to the backyard and poured the water into the washtub as her mother bent over the scrub board. It was heavy work, and working around the stove was sure enough hot, but it was not as hot and hard as working the tobacco field.

Lord knows, nothin's as hard as working the tobacco field.

Addie recalled how her mother took her to the fields starting when she was too young to do much more than pull worms off the tobacco plants. Then as she got older, she had joined the rest of the family at their work.

Bent over plants all day—the sun beating down on your back—settin' the plants in the spring and suckerin' in the summer. Cuttin' leaves in the fall.

Addie shook her head.

But the ironing, that was easier. Her mother let Addie start out with handkerchiefs, then petticoats, until she was sure enough with the iron. Shirts were last. When her mother was sure she could move the hot iron quickly enough over the heavily starched collars, she let her take on the shirts.

"You gotta move that iron fast when there's starch in the shirts," Laura Scott taught her, standing behind her youngest daughter and looking over her shoulder as she worked. "Move that iron so you don't scorch 'em. Come on now, push it fast!"

Turned out Addie was good at it. So good that, as a teenager, Addie told her mother she was going to quit the tobacco patch and find full-time work doing laundry.

She found steady work at one or another of the white board-inghouses in town doing laundry and housekeeping. She liked the work well enough, and the women she worked for, widows who took in boarders, treated her fine. The boarders, always men, did not trouble her either. While they never touched her, early on she learned to ignore the talk . . . the white men's talk. They mostly kept their voices low when she was around. But sometimes, especially if they were gathered in the sitting room smoking their cigars and drinking whiskey, they loosened up when they talked about the colored women. Their "colored gals," they called them. Addie heard names.

Callie.

Dosie.

Birdie Mae.

Those and others—they were common enough names that she might have known these women, or no. But she ignored the talk, kept her head down, finished her work, and left the room.

Before Mrs. Beatty, Addie had worked for another widow for quite a few years before the woman closed the boardinghouse. The woman told her the house had termites and one day was sure to come tumbling down and that she was going to go live with a sister in Memphis before that happened. But Addie heard around town that she ran off with one of her boarders. Before the woman left, she made a reference for Addie to work for Mrs. Beatty. Mrs. Beatty hired her and that was when Addie's life changed.

Addie gasped as the next spasm came full on, but this time the pressure was in her lower back. She arched forward. The pain gripped her. "Good God, what's taking that man so long," Addie hissed between her teeth. Then she felt wet between her legs. She lifted herself and pulled the folds of her dress out from under her. She looked down and moaned. It was blood.

"Oh no," she said. "Oh no!"

She heard Mrs. Beatty's high-pitched voice. "The horse is over at the stable, Mr. Mitchell . . ."

"Then send your boy for it, Mrs. Beatty," Tom answered sharply. "Would you please?"

Addie panted as the pain slowly went away. Mrs. Beatty was still chattering downstairs. Addie could no longer hear Tom's voice.

Would this be happening if I had never come to work for Mrs. Beatty?

Then she felt the baby move, turning inside her.

"Hold on, child," she whispered. "Hold on."

☙

A few weeks after Mrs. Beatty hired her, Addie had just closed the door to a boarder's room and walked over to the top of the stairs, carrying a basket of laundry. She stood there and watched as Mrs. Beatty waited at the door, ready to greet her boarders, as she did most evenings.

"Good evening, Mr. Mitchell," Mrs. Beatty said with a short curtsy, a wide grin spread across her face. "Welcome home, sir."

She was a widow. Addie had heard it whispered around Clarksville that Mrs. Beatty's husband must have left gold buried somewhere in their backyard because she was one of the few people around Clarksville and in Montgomery County proper who actually seemed to prosper after the war. Even though she took in boarders, which was usually a sign of hard times, she entertained lavishly. An invitation to one of her Sunday afternoon teas was coveted by any number of white women of means in town. Mrs. Beatty often asked Addie to come in on those Sundays and help serve the guests.

Mrs. Beatty was a large-boned woman and wore a huge bustle—a kind that had not been worn by most women for almost twenty years. Addie held back a grin as she started down the stairs and watched as Mr. Mitchell tried to steer clear of her, bustle and all, while entering the house. He took a quick step back and removed his hat, held out his arm, and motioned for her to enter the foyer before him as he said, "Good evening, Mrs. Beatty. Fine evening at that." Then he walked past Mrs. Beatty and headed toward the stairs.

Addie was almost halfway down the stairs when Mrs. Beatty looked up at her and said sharply, "Addie, make way for Mr. Mitchell. Did you clean his room? Are those his shirts?"

"Yes—no, ma'am. This basket . . ." She was flustered as she tried to hurry down the steps, answer Mrs. Beatty, and steer clear of Mr. Mitchell at the same time. The heel of her shoe caught the edge of the worn rug that was tacked to the steps. Still holding the basket with her left hand, she let go of the basket with her right hand and grabbed the banister to keep from falling.

"Yes, ma'am, I cleaned his room. These are Mr. Bradley's shirts, ma'am," she said, still steadying herself. "Mr. Mitchell's shirts are already hanging on the line."

Mr. Mitchell looked straight at her as he made his way up the steps. He seemed to be watching her every move. Addie knew she should look away. There was no question about that, him being a white man. But he was staring her down, strong, and she felt that she had no choice but to return his gaze. She glanced aside as they passed each other.

When Addie reached the bottom of the stairs, Mrs. Beatty cleared her throat and said, "Mr. Mitchell, you be sure and let me know if your collars need more starch."

"I'll do that," he answered from the top of the stairs.

Mrs. Beatty grabbed Addie's arm, stopping her as she walked past. Addie looked down at her basket of laundry as Mrs. Beatty spoke. "Girl, Mr. Tom Mitchell's grandfather was Senator Thomas, Senator Gustavus Thomas—one of the finest men in the government of our grand Confederacy. Why, Senator Thomas was a schoolmate of our President Jefferson Davis. And Mr. Mitchell is esteemed in his own right: he's an attorney and the youngest man to be admitted to the Tennessee bar." She paused and then added solicitously, "You take special care with Mr. Mitchell's collars, hear me?"

"Yes, ma'am," Addie said, still looking down at her basket. Mrs. Beatty let go of her arm, and Addie hurried away toward the back of the house.

Several days later, in the late afternoon, Addie arrived at Tom Mitchell's door at the end of the hallway to clean his room. She knocked perfunctorily and, not expecting him to be there because it was not yet evening, she walked right in. Addie gasped when she saw Tom Mitchell sitting at his desk. She almost dropped the basket she held in her hand.

If Mrs. Beatty finds out one of her boarders was still in his room when I entered . . .

Addie quickly blurted out an apology, "I'm . . . I'm sorry, Mr. Mitchell. I'll come back later." She immediately backed out of the room, ready to close the door.

"Nonsense," Tom Mitchell said, putting his pen in the inkwell as he spoke, "you don't have to do that. You can straighten things up while I'm here. I'll be working at my desk."

"Yes, sir," she said. She glanced over her shoulder and looked down the hall to see if anyone was watching her, but no one was there. She reentered his room, closing the door behind her.

Addie tried to work as if she were alone in the room. She bent across his bed and pulled the sheets taut, tucking them in tightly at the corners. She shook out his quilt and then spread it across the bed and in between the bedposts. She took the feather duster from the basket and lightly brushed over his dresser and nightstand.

Addie did not dare look over at Tom Mitchell as he sat at his desk. But she did not have to look at him to know that even though he was sitting there, he was not working: She could feel the force of his gaze upon her while she worked. He was staring at her while she moved about his room, and she knew it. She finished her work as quickly as she could. She just wanted to get out of that room and away from that man.

Alone with a white man in one of her rooms . . . I just hope Mrs. Beatty never finds out. She'll have my job for sure.

She quickly gathered Tom Mitchell's clothes up off the floor—his shirt and collar, his nightshirt and drawers—and filled the basket.

There . . . now, I'm finished.

She felt a wave of relief.

Then, looking down at her basket, Addie walked toward the door. But just as she started to pass Tom Mitchell, he reached out from where he sat in his chair and grabbed her arm firmly.

Addie gasped and briefly held her breath, her eyes fixed on the basket. *Oh my God!*

Her body tensed.

What's he gonna do, what's he gonna do to me?

"I'm sorry. Really, I am. I'm not gonna hurt you," Tom Mitchell said, as if reading her mind.

Addie still looked down at the basket. She was breathing quickly.

"Look at me, Addie," he said softly, as if to coax her.

She still looked away.

"I said, look at me!" He spoke deliberately, now.

She raised her eyes from her basket and turned her head over toward him. Their eyes met.

"Are you afraid of me?" he asked. He relaxed his hold on her arm.

"Yes. No . . . I don't know, sir," she answered, her chest heaving with each breath.

Addie was frightened.

Tom Mitchell let his hand drop from her arm. He stood up and cupped her face in his hands, looking deep into her eyes as she looked up at him. She cringed inside at the touch of his hands on her face.

"Don't be afraid," he said soothingly. "I won't hurt you. Fact is, I think you're the prettiest thing I've ever laid eyes on. Thought so from the time I saw you trip on those steps with your basket of laundry." He smiled.

"Come on up here tomorrow when you finish your wash," he said. "Come up around this time, before the others come home. No one will know you're here."

As Addie listened, she realized he was not going to do anything to her right then and her breathing slowed down. But she remained silent. She felt as if she couldn't speak.

"You hear me?" he asked.

There was more silence. Tom dropped his hands from her face but held her gaze.

So this is how it happens. And now, now it's happening to me.

There was only one answer that she could give. She knew that.

"Yes," Addie answered, her voice almost a whisper. "Yes, sir."

Addie broke the gaze and stepped away, quickly carrying her basket to the door. Tom followed close behind her. He stood in the doorway as she left the room. She heard his door close as she reached the top of the stairs.

Addie hurried down the stairs.

He was waitin' for me . . . He knew I would be comin' to clean his room. He came home early and he was waitin' . . .

Then she almost tripped as she caught her heel on the rug on the same step she had stumbled on just a few days earlier. The stumble brought her back to the work at hand.

I can't think anymore about this just now. I have work to do before I can go home. I have to wash Mr. Mitchell's laundry. I have to hang out his clothes.

She steadied herself on the remaining steps and then walked to the washtub behind the house.

Walking home toward Colored Town, Addie did think about it.

So this is how it happens.

She had seen any number of married couples—a brown-skinned woman and a brown- or dark brown–skinned man—with a yellow or high-yellow toddler in hand. Yes, there were whispers, but folks always attributed the light color to Indian blood. "That's the Indian blood coming out," they would say. "Lots of mingling of Indians and coloreds in years past around Montgomery County." Folks nodded and acknowledged.

But this is how it happens . . .

Addie felt a cramp in her stomach. She felt sick. She wanted to talk to someone. And she wanted to say more than just "Fine evenin'" and "Good evenin'" to folks she passed in Colored Town on the way home. She turned down her street, Franklin Street, and saw her parents' house up ahead, a couple of blocks before her own home. She wanted to talk to her mother about what had happened. But what would she say?

"Mama, Mrs. Beatty's boarder told me to come back to his room tomorrow!"

And what would her mother say? "The nerve of that man. Why, I'll have your father go over there and give him a piece of his mind. Imagine that white man, from an upstanding family at that, talkin' to my daughter like that!"

Addie caught herself before she laughed out loud just as she passed her parents' house. No one was sitting out on the porch and the front door was closed.

Order of the Camellia would have Daddy strung up from a tree by nightfall for sure if he went over there to Mr. Mitchell talkin' like that!

As she saw her front porch from a distance, she focused her thoughts closer to home. Willie. He would be getting home from the Shelby farm later that evening. And he was the one person she could never tell.

"He must never know," she whispered under her breath.

She and Willie Jackson had been married for about two years now. No children. Addie was beginning to think she was barren. And if Mr. Mitchell had his way with her, she hoped she was.

Good Lord, how could this be happening to me?

She came in full sight of her house.

Well I can't think anymore about it right now. I just can't. I have to get dinner started so it'll be warm in the oven when Willie gets home. I'll cook up some collard greens . . . add some bits of smoked ham. I don't think I have enough cornmeal left to make another batch of muffins, but biscuits will do. Yes, I'll just whip up some biscuits.

She walked up the porch steps to her front door and went inside.

"Where do you think you're headed? You told me your work's finished for the day!"

Addie was midway up the steps when she heard Mrs. Beatty's shrill reprimand.

"Ma'am, I . . ." Addie said as she turned to face Mrs. Beatty.

"Don't you ma'am me. I have a good mind—"

"I don't like being disturbed like this, Mrs. Beatty." It was Tom Mitchell. Addie looked up at him from where she stood halfway up the stairs. He glared down from the top of the steps at Mrs. Beatty, who stood with one foot perched on the first step.

He nodded at Addie as she continued walking up toward the landing.

"Do you understand what I'm telling you, Mrs. Beatty?" Tom added tersely. By then, Addie was standing near him at the top of the stairs, looking down at Mrs. Beatty.

Mrs. Beatty stuttered, her tone of voice greatly subdued, "W-w-why . . . why y-yes, Mr. Mitchell. I-I understand. I understand perfectly." She turned to walk away. Then she stopped and looked up at Tom one more time. "I'm sorry to disturb you." She slowly bowed her head, then walked with an anxious pace toward the dining room.

Addie headed down the hallway. Tom followed her into his room and closed the door. "That old cow!" he said, leaning against the door. "She says she can charge more for the other rooms on account of who my granddaddy was. If this place wasn't so close to my office, I'd move tomorrow!" he said.

He stepped toward Addie. She stood next to his bed, staring down at the deep red leafy print of the Persian rug that covered most of the oak floor, waiting to see what would happen next. She wore a plain cotton shift, faded indigo with a starched, rounded white collar. Her hands hung low and were tightly clasped in front of her. Her chest heaved with each breath.

He moved over to the chair at his desk and sat down. "Addie," he said. She looked up, then he motioned with his head for her to sit on the settee next to the desk.

"You have such a pretty face, Addie," Tom said. He leaned toward her and touched her cheek with the back of his hand. Her whole body stiffened.

"Smile for me."

She curved her lips. Tom stroked her cheek.

"What do you think about that makes you smile?"

"I don't know, sir . . ."

"Sure you do," he said, still stroking her cheek.

"I guess my dog . . ."

"What's his name?"

"Sooner, sir."

"Why, Sooner?"

"I guess 'cause he'd sooner be one kinda dog as another." Addie smiled, a genuine smile this time, as she explained the name. "We don't know what he is."

"We?" Tom interrupted.

"My husband, sir," she answered and stopped smiling. "He named the dog."

Near the top of the stairs, sitting on the floor, leaning against the wall, Addie struggled through a spasm. She saw Tom Mitchell standing in the foyer and looking up at her through the railing posts. She moaned and gripped her belly.

"Addie?" he asked. "Are you all right up there? Tell me somethin', girl!" he said to her.

"Yes, I'm fine. But things are movin' along fast, now," Addie answered. She knew the signs from when Patsy was born: the deep, sharp pains, the blood. She knew her water bag would break next. She knew the baby was soon coming.

"Mrs. Beatty's boy is out on an errand. When he returns, she'll send him to the stable to get the horse and buggy. She reckoned—"

Addie hollered, gripped by a strong spasm, this one from deep in her belly. It was stronger than all the others. She wanted to tell him to get her home. Get her a midwife. Just get the baby born. "Oooh—aaargh!"

"Good God, Addie!" Tom said, almost simultaneously with her cry.

She could hear him as he bounded up the stairs.

"Jesus, Addie," he said as he rushed over to her and knelt, pulling her body over to him, resting her head against his chest. "You can't have this baby here, you just can't!"

"Nothin' . . . I can do about . . . when . . . when this baby decides to be born, Tom Mitchell . . . you know that," she said, panting again as she spoke.

"Listen, girl . . . I'll get you home. We just have to wait for Mrs. Beatty's boy, is all. She'll send him for the buggy as soon as he gets back."

"Calm down, now," he said, stroking her head. "I'll take care of you. You're my Addie, you know that. More than two years, now, since I saw you trip on that step . . . and you're still my dear Addie."

Addie moaned and squirmed in his arms.

"Addie, what do you think? Is this one a boy?" he asked, his voice almost a whisper.

Addie heard him but she could not answer. All she could think about was the pain as it subsided. She made a low panting sound.

"Jesus, if it's a boy . . ." Tom said, answering himself, "if it's a boy, I just might take my son over to Cumberland Hill and show him to my daddy . . ."

Addie squeezed his arm and gasped. "Tom Mitchell, you *are* gonna make me have this baby right here and now! You can't go takin' your colored baby boy over to Cumberland Hill, even if he does come out lookin' just 'bout white like Patsy. You think they'd let you raise a little colored boy as a Mitchell?" She moaned and squeezed his arm even harder.

"I don't think much of what I could do would put my daddy in any worse a state of mind than he's in right now. Hell, the war's been over twenty-five years now, and he's still talkin' about losing his cotton farm. 'Three hundred acres of some of the best low-hill land in middle Tennessee,' he still crows from that ol' creaky rocker of his. 'I was on the verge of raisin' a crop that'd set the market on fire . . .'"

He had told Addie different versions of this story before. She knew what was coming next. Tom would tell her how, when he was a young boy, his father vowed to get his mother and the children out of her father's house on Cumberland Hill and into their own home. How his mother told his father he'd never make any money off his farm until he hired some Negroes to work it. How his father reminded her that he had owned slaves before the war, and he'd be damned if he paid a darkie one penny to work his land.

But Addie did not care much what he was saying right then and there. She moaned louder and dug her nails deep into Tom's arm. He gripped her tightly.

"Mr. Mitchell! Mr. Mitchell!" It was Mrs. Beatty calling from the foyer.

Tom jumped up and leaned over the railing. "Yes, Mrs. Beatty?"

"My boy just returned with the buggy. They're both at your disposal," she said calmly.

Tom answered, "Thank you, Mrs. Beatty." Then he turned and looked down at Addie and muttered, "Thank God!"

Addie noticed Mrs. Beatty's tone of voice, polite now, with the baby coming and all. She recalled when Mrs. Beatty wasn't so polite, when she noticed that Addie was with child a second time. Mrs. Beatty looked down at her swollen belly and then up to her face and locked eyes with her. She said to her, with contempt in her voice, "Girl, you'd best be glad Mr. Mitchell comes from such an esteemed family. Otherwise, I'd have you out on the street. And I would make sure you never worked at another boardinghouse anywhere in Montgomery County," she said. "Just make sure you stay out of sight of the other boarders."

That same day, Addie told Tom what Mrs. Beatty had said.

"Don't worry about it. I'll take care of it," Tom said to Addie.

Addie didn't ask him what he'd said to Mrs. Beatty, but the woman never said another cross word to her. In fact, other than pleasantries, it seemed to Addie that Mrs. Beatty rarely said anything to her at all.

Addie felt another spasm coming and grabbed her belly. She tried to get up on her own, but she couldn't.

"Tom! I don't think . . ."

He bent down, hooked his arms under her armpits, and pulled her up. As he reached down to grab the quilt, Addie buckled over. She yelled in pain.

"I got you, girl. Now, come on."

He leaned over and scooped her up in his arms, wrapping the quilt around her in the same movement. As he stood holding her, he looked down at the deep red blood stain on the rug. "So much blood," he whispered, "so much blood."

Addie tensed in his arms. She moaned.

"Shush now, girl," he murmured in Addie's ear as he walked them to the stairway. She rested her head against his shoulder.

Addie felt how tentatively he walked as he slowly made his way down the stairs, stopping once to lean his hip against the banister as she shifted her weight in his arms. When he reached the foyer and turned toward the back of the house, Addie lifted her head from his shoulder and noticed that Mrs. Beatty was standing by the doorway to the kitchen, arms folded across her bosom. Addie turned her head so that she would not have to make eye contact with Mrs. Beatty.

"Mr. Mitchell, with all due respect to you and your esteemed family, I run a respectable boardinghouse and—"

"Not now, Mrs. Beatty, not now!"

At the back of the house, Mrs. Beatty's boy was sitting in the box seat, reins in hand, ready to drive the carriage. He looked straight ahead.

Tom lifted Addie up into the back seat. She held onto his arm and looked directly into his eyes as he tucked the quilt around her and got her settled in.

As he pulled away, he whispered, "I wish I could see you home."

Addie knew that could never happen. And if Willie were there when she got home, he would see the state she was in and leave. Addie was sure of it. That's what he'd done after her first child was born. He was there when Addie's birth pains started. He even went to fetch the midwife. But after Patsy was born and the baby's color never came in, he just up and left. He came back when her laying up time was over. He barely looked at her once she began showing she was with child again.

Tom looked at her and whispered, "Addie, my dear Addie."

She tensed up, gripped by another wave of pain. Tom reached over and pulled her hand from his arm. Then he raised her hand up to his mouth, held it to his lips, and kissed it. Addie was stunned. She was afraid to look around her to see if Mrs. Beatty or one of the boarders had seen what Tom Mitchell had just done. For a moment, she forgot about the pain.

She cringed at the thought of what could happen to her if some white folk saw that and word got out. She felt the tightness of the spasm once more.

Tom took her hand from his lips and put it down on top of the quilt. He reached out and slapped the hind side of the stallion. Looking up at the boy, he ordered him, "Take her home to 524 Franklin Street!"

"Wait, a midwife—I need the midwife!" Addie leaned forward, gripping the quilt that covered her belly.

Hurriedly, he told the boy, "After you take her home, you go fetch the midwife, you hear?"

"Yes, sir," the boy said, still looking straight ahead. The boy snapped the reins, and Addie was gone.

2

1894

FIRE

"Come along, girls," Addie Jackson said as she stepped back and took Patsy and Dorothy May each by the hand after they had stopped to stare, jaws dropped, at the man in the red suit. After smiling and saying, "Hello, Deacon Thompson," to the man who had caught her daughters' attention, she pulled them along as she whispered, "Don't stare. You know the deacon."

Addie understood that Patsy and Dorothy May had stopped to gaze at Mr. Thompson not because they knew him as a deacon at their church, Mt. Zion Baptist, but because today they saw him dressed as the grand marshal of the Colored Town Fourth of July parade. While he had led the processional most years past, this time he had outdone himself with his finery: he was wearing a white top hat and a crimson tailcoat with matching trousers while holding up an American flag with his right arm and carrying an oversized walking stick in his left hand.

"Why is he dressed like that, Mama?" Patsy asked.

"He's the grand marshal. He leads the parade," their mother answered.

"But, Mama, why—" Dorothy May asked softly.

Addie cut her off. "It's a celebration, dear child. Look around—don't you see how everyone is dressed in their Sunday best?" she answered as they walked up to the center of the Montgomery County fairgrounds, where everyone who would be marching that day gathered to take their place. "Look," she said, nodding toward the men wearing colored shirts beneath their waistcoats and then at women and girls wearing blouses with high, lace-trimmed collars.

"This is a big day in Colored Town. Bigger than Christmas, I'd say," their mother continued. "I'm so proud of my girls, your first time marching in the parade and all."

Addie had made her daughters white blouses with leg-of-mutton sleeves, like the ones she had seen at the Emporium, the one store in Colored Town that always seemed to carry the latest fashions. She did not dare tell her girls this, but she had copied the style not only so that they would be festively dressed, though that was a big part of the reason, for sure. But she also did it so that maybe, just maybe, the ladies who were sure to come up to Patsy and Dorothy May after the parade would comment on how stylishly they were dressed and not just make a fuss over their long braids and "good hair" as happened so often at church and other places.

I know what they're thinking when they fuss over my girls' hair. I know what's on their minds when they take a braid in their hand and say, What a nice grade of hair your girls have, Addie, really nice . . . And all the while looking over at my head of hair. Colored hair. Ornery hair. Looking at it pulled back in a bun or braided close to my head like I do with a hat on top on Sundays. I know what they're thinking when they say, That Indian blood's coming through in your girls, I suspect? Why I bet you enjoy sitting in the evening and brushing their nice long hair, don't you . . . Um-hum, I know what they're thinking. They're thinking about Tom Mitchell. I know that. Well just let them think what they want. Just go on and think what they want.

Addie looked around for the banner for the Mt. Zion Baptist Church children's Sunday school class. Each group taking part in the parade procession carried a paper banner displaying their name.

"There," she said to the girls, changing her train of thought and pointing over to her left a few yards. "There's the banner for your Sunday school class. Look, there're the other children. I see your teacher, too."

At the sight of their friends, the girls tried to pull away from their mother and run toward them. Still holding their hands, Addie held them back.

"Listen, girls, now you listen to me," Addie said, kneeling in front of them. "Patsy, you hold your sister's hand and don't let go. You hear me?" she said.

"Yes, Mama," Patsy said.

"And, Dorothy May, you mind your sister, you hear me?" Addie said.

"Yes, Mama," Dorothy May repeated.

"And both of you, stay with your Sunday school class. I'll see you at the end of the parade, at the picnic grounds. I'm going over there to help the other ladies set out the food once I go back home and pick up that corn and fried chicken."

Addie leaned forward and kissed them both on the forehead.

"Now, scoot!" she said letting go their hands. Still kneeling, she watched them run off.

Addie knew it would be a long while, and the tables laden with food, before the parade made its way from the fairgrounds to the picnic grounds, but she hurried just the same. She took a shortcut to Colored Town that took her just outside of downtown Clarksville. It was a less traveled part of the city, so she knew she would make better time getting home without having to make polite small talk with colored folks she might meet or having to step into the street for any white folks she might pass on the sidewalk. She could stay focused on getting home and on what she had to do when she got there: pick up the muslin sack she had filled with dozens of ears of corn—she had been shucking corn late into the night before—and then get the basket full of the fried chicken she had been cooking since early morning. She had killed two of her fat hens at dawn, wrung their necks before the girls woke up. The girls couldn't stand the sight of her killing a bird.

But they love to eat that fried chicken . . . Guess they forget the killing part once it gets on their plate.

Addie chuckled softly to herself before she thought of the work she had yet to do.

She hoped her husband would be there to help her carry the food she had prepared to the picnic grounds.

If Willie's not there, I'll just have to make two trips.

She shook her head. When he'd left the house that morning, he hadn't said one way or the other whether he'd be at the picnic or even at the parade.

Lord, Lord, this is going to be such a long day . . .

Then she saw him. Addie stopped, dead in her tracks. He was still quite a distance away, but she was sure it was him. She recognized his gait, the way he favored his left leg, and the way he gestured with his hands. He was walking next to someone, a man, and he was making a point, pointing at the ground with his index finger, as he liked to do.

It was Tom Mitchell. Dressed in his waistcoat and bowler hat—same as the other gentleman—and one of the shirts she had starched and ironed for him the day before. He was surely on his way to take his place on the parade viewing stand with the other dignitaries. He had just been elected Tennessee's attorney general. "At twenty-six years of age, the youngest on record ever elected to that esteemed post," he had read to Addie from the newspaper column with pride in his voice. Addie knew he would be sitting with the mayor, judges, and other elected officials.

Addie started walking again, moving toward him. But as she stepped, she felt sweat beading up on her forehead. Her armpits were dripping wet, and it wasn't from the late-morning heat. She thought her heart would pound clear through her chest. She knew what was about to happen: Tom Mitchell would expect her to stay on the sidewalk as he and the other man passed, like any white woman would, walking down the sidewalk. He had made that good and clear to her shortly after Dorothy May was born.

"My God," Addie said out loud when she realized how much time had passed. "It was four years ago."

It had happened a few weeks after Dorothy May was born. Addie had walked the girls over to her parents' house—her mother took in laundry so that she could watch the girls—and then headed over to the boardinghouse. She was nearly there when she saw Tom Mitchell turn the corner. He was walking toward her, probably on his way to the courthouse. When she was a few steps away from him, she automatically stopped and stepped off the curb and into the street, her gaze lowered so as not to make eye contact. When she saw his feet pass by, she stepped back up and went on her way. It was what colored folks did when they passed any white person. She didn't even give it another thought until he came up to his room later on, toward evening.

Addie had been standing at his window as she often did. Curtains pulled back, she looked out and waited for him to make his way home. Sure enough, she saw him come around the corner. She saw him walk up the street. But when he reached Mrs. Beatty's place, he didn't glance up to catch a glimpse of her like he usually did before entering the house. No, he walked straight to the door.

Addie heard his footsteps as he strode up the stairs and made his way down the hall. His steps sounded heavier than usual.

He's had a bad day, that's all it is.

She turned toward the door. He walked into the room and slammed the door shut. He didn't greet her as he usually did. There was no, "My Addie." There was no smile. He dropped his satchel down by his desk.

"Don't do that again," was all he said, glaring at her as she stood by the window.

She was confused. "What? What are you talking about?" she asked.

"I'm talking about what you did this morning when you passed me on your way here."

"N-n-no! You can't mean . . . why I just . . ."

"You see me, you walk by me on the sidewalk like any respectable woman, you hear me?" he said. "On the sidewalk!"

"Tom Mitchell, you've lived in this town as long as I have. You know the way of it—"

"You do as I say," he said, cutting her off.

"But you know what could happen to me if anyone saw that. Why if word got to the Order of the Camellia or any one of those white fellas, I'd be strung up a tree and you know it. The girls, why one of those men might—"

Tom quickly stepped toward Addie. She flinched as he grabbed her arm tightly. He spoke slowly and deliberately. "You listen to me," he said. "If anyone so much as tries to lay a hand on you or the girls . . . If anyone tries to hurt you or the girls in any way, I'll kill 'em."

He let go Addie's arm. She stood there, stunned.

"You expect me to cross the color line," she said.

"Seems to me, we'll both be crossing it," he said.

"But it's me and the girls who'll—"

"You're the mother of my girls, not some common Negress," he answered, before she could finish her sentence. "I won't have you stepping into the street when I pass. I won't have it! I said no harm will come to you, and I mean it." Then he turned and walked over to his desk. "Now you do as I say," he said as he sat down.

Addie stood there, trying to make sense of what he was telling her to do.

Good God, if I do this, what'll folks say?

She knew good and well what the talk already was in Colored Town. Her mother had long before told her the whispering that was going on around the church about her and "those high-yellow girls." Addie figured white folks were whispering the same thing, what with Mrs. Beatty keeping up the gossip on her end.

I guess the only difference is, now there'll be no doubt, no doubt in anybody's mind, colored or white. And he knows that.

She stared over at Tom. Then made her way over to the settee and sat down. She watched him as he shuffled through some papers. She took in a deep breath and slowly let it out.

He says no harm will come to me or the girls. Well then, I guess I'll find out sure enough just how much power the Mitchell and Thomas names really do carry around this town.

From that day on, even though Addie didn't pass Tom very often as she walked about Clarksville, the few times she did, she obeyed him and walked by him on the sidewalk, like every other white woman around town would do. He never tipped his hat. He never went that far. And she never looked his way so as to make eye contact. She was not bold enough to do that. But she walked by him—on the sidewalk—just as he said to. Other folks were around when it happened, and they had to have seen it. She was sure they did. But no one said a word—at least not to her. And Tom kept his word: no harm had come to her or the girls.

But that day in 1894, the day of the Colored Town Fourth of July parade, was different. On that day, Tom Mitchell wasn't alone as he walked down the sidewalk. He was walking with another man. And that was what made Addie sweat like blood and her heart pound hard. It was one thing for Tom to make her ignore the color line. Here, she knew full well it was something else—bordering on madness—for Tom to think he could make another white man do the same thing. Yet as she drew closer, she could tell that was exactly what Tom planned to do.

"Tom Mitchell has lost his natural mind," Addie muttered to herself as she made herself put one foot in front of the other. She did not want any trouble. While she could hear Tom's voice telling her he would protect her and the girls from a riled-up mob, he didn't live in Colored Town. He wouldn't be there, waiting just inside the front door with a shotgun at the ready, at the first sign of trouble. He could promise all he liked, but in the end, she knew it would be her and her two girls against some spittin' angry white folks in Clarksville when it came down to it.

There. Before she knew it, she was face-to-face with Mr. Thomas Mitchell and the gentleman walking next to him. Addie looked Tom in the eyes as she walked by on the sidewalk; she couldn't help herself. Tom met her gaze. But she didn't dare look at the other man. She could see that Tom moved to the side, ever so slightly, to make way for her as she passed. Her chest heaved. She thought she would lose the little breakfast she'd had time to eat that morning before heading out with Patsy and Dorothy May. Then they were past her. She heard the other man speak, clear as day, as the two of them walked away.

"Good God, Tom," the man said, "have you lost hold of your senses? Why didn't you just go and tip your hat to her?"

"Is there a problem?" Tom asked calmly.

"Yes, I'd say there's a problem!" the man replied. "This is a dangerous game you're playing, Tom Mitchell, making a fool of yourself over this colored woman."

They were a good distance away by now. The man's voice trailed off. But Addie heard that much and a bit more.

"I wouldn't want one of the boys from the Order of the Camellia to get wind of how she walked by us like that."

Addie stopped in her tracks. She took a deep breath. "Lord have mercy," she said out loud, "and please protect my girls and me." Then she continued on her way home.

Out of the corner of her eye, Addie kept looking for Patsy and Dorothy May to come around that final turn of the parade procession and onto the picnic grounds. The men—about fifty of them it seemed to her—from the Middle Tennessee Colored Agricultural and Mechanical Association had just come marching in. They marched right on over to the tables where Addie and women from the different churches around town had just about finished setting out the main dishes—fried chicken, corn on the cob, cornbread, biscuits, and fried green tomatoes. They put out more corn as Sister Ferguson finished roasting the ears over a nearby pit fire. On another table, there were platters stacked against platters of other food, each heaped with the women's various specialties.

"Shoo, you men go on now!" It was Sister Mayfield, talking to the men as they began to crowd around the tables.

"The meal won't be served until the parade is over and one of these pastors around here blesses the food. You know that. So, you might as well just go on and find a shady spot and sit yourselves down. Go on now!" she said.

The men took their time walking away. Sister Mayfield looked over at Addie. "Your girls will be along presently," she said to her.

"What's that?" Addie asked as she turned and looked over at the woman.

"I see you looking over that way, watching for your girls. They'll be here in no time."

"You're right, Sister Mayfield. You're right," Addie said, smiling. "It's just that if I'd have known that this parade was going to take this long, I would've made the girls wear their sun bonnets. The sun's beating down somethin' fierce."

"Afraid they'll show up looking like field hands, are you?" someone said from behind her.

Addie's back stiffened. She turned and looked to see who'd said it: a woman she barely knew. She'd seen her at church now and then, but not enough to even know her name. Before she could decide if she should just ignore the woman or get up in her face and say something back, someone else squealed, "Why looky here, my my my . . ."

The ladies at the table looked over at the woman walking toward them.

One of them said, "Sister James has brought a jar of her pickled pigs' feet. Looks like a gallon jar at that. Now it's really a picnic for sure!"

Sister James broke out in a wide grin as she walked toward them.

"Now you ladies know I promised you I'd bring in a jar. One of the last ones left from hog-killing time last year. I've been saving it just for today. Had to hide it from that husband of mine or he'd of finished 'em off for sure, um-hum," she said, setting the jar down on the table next to the platters of chicken.

"Well we'll see how long it takes before that jar gets empty today!" Sister Mayfield said, laughing.

Addie laughed, then stood and talked with the other women, all the while keeping an eye out for her girls. She knew the parade would be ending soon because she saw a caravan of carriages arrive carrying the Negro dignitaries who had been seated in the viewing stand. Riding in the carriages were ministers and their wives, teachers, fraternal officers, and Republican Party activists. The ladies had parasols opened to shield themselves from the heat of the sun. The dignitaries stepped out of the carriages and began to organize themselves into a receiving line where they would greet the parade participants and picnickers.

The parade procession trickled in, now with the group from the Young Men's Christian Association. As she peered beyond that crowd of men, still looking for her girls, Addie heard a brass band from a distance. But before the band arrived, the Mt. Zion Baptist Church children's Sunday school class appeared around the bend. She breathed a sigh of relief as she looked among the youngsters for Patsy and Dorothy May. She did not have to look for long because the sisters broke rank and ran toward her, squealing, "Mama, we were in the parade! We were in the parade!"

Addie kneeled and scooped them up in her arms. "Oh, yes you were! And I'm so proud of you!"

"Mama, we're hungry! When can we eat? Can we have some fried chicken?" The girls spoke at the same time, both looking in the direction of the tables piled high with food.

"Not yet. You know we have to wait until the food is blessed. Then you have to wait your turn until we prepare plates for all of the dignitaries. Look over there at that receiving line. They'll be busy greeting people for a long time, and we don't want to run out of food before they have a chance to sit and eat."

Folks were already lined up, eager to shake hands with the colored ministers and officials.

"But, look here . . . it's such a hot day and you've been such good girls, if you promise to sit still and wait your turn for dinner, I think I can get each of you a nice, cool glass of lemonade. How would you like that?" she asked.

"Yes, Mama, yes! We promise!" they squealed.

"Now, shhhh!" Addie said. "Wait right here. I'll be right back."

As Addie stood up, she looked beyond the receiving line and saw a carriage approaching with one passenger. It was a white man. It took her but an instant to see that it was Tom Mitchell.

She knew that it was honor enough for him, the attorney general and a statewide elected official, to be there in the stands viewing the parade. Almost as good as the governor himself. But to come to the picnic grounds afterwards . . .

Never happened before, not to my recollection.

The white officials honored the occasion and watched the parade, but none had ever accepted an invitation to attend the picnic and stand at the head of the receiving line. She chuckled to herself as she watched the ministers almost tripping over themselves rushing to greet Tom and escort him to his place in the line.

Addie felt a tug at her skirt. "Mama, the lemonade," Patsy pleaded.

"Yes child, here I go. Here I go," she said as she turned.

As Addie left to get the lemonade, she noticed that the women around the food table had stopped what they were doing and were straining their necks to see Tom Mitchell take his place among the colored folk. But they quickly turned and busied themselves with nothing in particular when Addie walked by.

When Addie returned carefully holding three glasses of lemonade, Dorothy May ran up to her. "Mama, what took you so long?" she asked.

"Lots of folks in line for lemonade on a hot day like today. Took me a long time to get to the front of the line," Addie answered. "But here you go." She carefully bent down so that each girl could take a glass. They started gulping their drinks.

"Hold on, now," Addie said as she straightened up. "Take your time. It's a hot day and all, but don't make yourselves sick," she said to them.

As she put the glass to her mouth, she watched Tom Mitchell shake hands with a few of the ministers who stood next to him as if saying goodbye. He stepped away from the receiving line and wiped his brow while removing his hat. Then he looked up and over to where Addie and the girls stood. She lowered her glass.

Good Lord, don't tell me he came to this picnic on the chance that he might see Patsy and Dorothy May . . . When was the last time he saw the girls?

Addie's heart began to pound. Before she knew what she was doing, Addie bent down and took the glass from Dorothy May's hand.

"But Mama, I'm not finished!" the girl said.

"Shush, now, I'll give it right back," Addie said, "but you take this glass here and give it to that white man over there standing next to the receiving line."

Addie handed Dorothy May the full glass of lemonade. "Go on now. And be careful you don't spill it."

Addie watched Dorothy May carefully hold the glass as she walked toward Tom. Addie looked up and saw that Tom was watching the girl as well. When Dorothy May reached him, only then did Addie look about her to see who else might be watching. But folks were busy talking and finding their seats at the picnic tables or making their way to the line. The officials in the receiving line kept shaking hands and did not seem to notice.

Or at least they had enough sense to mind their own business.

Addie watched as Tom Mitchell leaned over, smiled, and took the glass from his daughter. He said something to her before she turned and skipped back toward Addie. He briefly made eye contact with Addie, then put the glass to his lips.

"Sister Ferguson, did you just see that? Why, if I hadn't seen it with my own eyes . . . she had that child take a glass of lemonade . . ."

It was Sister Mayfield. She hadn't tried to lower her voice, and Addie heard every word that came out of her mouth. Addie turned her head toward the table where the two women stood and stared straight at both of them.

"It's nothing, nothing at all," Sister Mayfield said to Sister Ferguson as she saw the look in Addie's eyes. Sister Mayfield quickly turned and hurried off.

Addie knew some version of the story was well on its way to being spread throughout the picnic grounds.

Everyone knows Sister Mayfield is just an old gossip, and there's not a thing I can do about it.

"Mama, can I finish my lemonade now?" It was Dorothy May. Addie leaned toward her daughter and placed the glass back in her hand. "A little bit spilled before I got to the man, but not much," the girl said as she reached up for her own glass. "He said to tell you thank you kindly."

"Who is that man, Mama?" Patsy asked.

"He's from an important family in Clarksville," Addie answered, looking down at Patsy. "And I gave him the lemonade because it's a very hot day."

By the time Addie looked back toward Tom, he had placed the glass on a nearby table and was headed toward his carriage.

"Come along, now," Addie said as she put a hand on each girl's shoulder. "Let's find a table where you can wait until the food is served."

As she turned with the girls and surveyed the available picnic tables, she almost gasped. There, standing over beyond the tables by a big oak tree, was Willie. He was glaring at her.

"Look, there's Daddy!" Patsy said.

"Where?" Dorothy May asked.

"Right there," Patsy said, pointing over to where he stood. Then she asked, "Mama, where's Daddy going?"

Willie Jackson had turned and was walking away from the picnic grounds.

"I don't know child, I don't know," Addie answered.

෨෮

"I can always tell when he's had his way with you," Willie Jackson said as he came in the front door and strode over to where Addie sat in the kitchen. He was not a big man, but he had a heavy walk. The room vibrated with each step across the worn, wooden floor.

He confronted her as she worked at the kitchen table. Addie was shelling peas. She put the peapods down on the table and put her head in her hands.

"Walking around town with your head up like you's white," he started ranting. "Sending Dorothy May over to him with that lemonade." He leaned across the table, put his hand under her chin, and pulled her head up. "Don't you think everybody saw that?"

Addie pulled her head away. She knew folks—even Willie—had seen her send Dorothy May over to Tom Mitchell with the lemonade. She knew there would be whispers behind her back. Sister Mayfield for one. But that was part of her life, had been since Patsy was born—the stares, the gossip.

"What're folks s'posed to think? What're folks s'posed to think about *me*? *I'm* s'posed to be your husband, but my two girls look white! Where'd that come from, eh? It sure didn't come from me." He held his hand up to her face. Then he grabbed her hand and turned it over in his own. "You aren't as dark as me—but you're still good and brown. None of his white's rubbed off on you yet . . ."

"Willie, you've been drinkin'," Addie said when she finally spoke, not trying to hide the disgust in her voice. She knew he would be drunk when he came home from the picnic. He always took to drink whenever he saw Tom Mitchell.

"No, I haven't been drinkin'," he said, leaning into her face. "Do you think the only time I talk 'bout him is when I been drinkin'? You don't think I'm man enough to talk 'bout him when I'm sober?"

Willie reached back his right arm and, with full force, slapped her across the face. Addie shrieked; the force of the blow almost knocked her out of her seat. She cowered in her chair with her head between her arms. He had never hit her before.

"Is that man enough for you?" Willie hissed at her.

He turned and stormed out of the kitchen. Addie heard him slam the front door as he left the house. She sat up in her chair, leaned her head back, and cried. The left side of her face throbbed where he had struck her. A few minutes later, she heard Patsy and Dorothy May skipping into the house from the back door. They were giggling between themselves. Addie quickly wiped her eyes with her sleeve. Her cheek was still hot, and she hoped Willie's slap hadn't left a mark on her face.

"Where's Daddy?" Dorothy May asked as she walked over to her mother and looked around the kitchen. "I thought I heard him talking in the kitchen."

Addie turned and looked down at her younger daughter.

"I don't know, honey," she said, trying to steady her voice. "He'll be back for dinner, I'm sure."

She turned and looked over at Patsy, "Help me shell these peas, here, and we'll have them tomorrow." Patsy sat next to her mother and helped her work. Dorothy May stood to the side and watched them both.

༄

Late that same night, Addie awoke to the smell of smoke, like a woodstove burning in the middle of the night.

Then she heard the piercing screams. She bolted out of bed and threw open her bedroom door. She stepped out into the living room and saw the walls covered with flames. She was blinded with the brightness of the fire. She coughed as smoke began to fill her lungs. "Oh God! Oh, my God!" she cried out.

The screams continued. Addie yelled, "Patsy! Dorothy May! Where are you?"

Using her forearm to shield her face from the smoke and the brightness of the flames, Addie sped to the corner of the living room where the girls slept on a single cot. Patsy was crouched on the smoldering wooden floor at the foot of the bed. She scooped Patsy up in her arms. She put the girl's face close to her breast to shield her from the smoke and heat. Still the screams continued. "Dorothy May!" she cried.

"Mama!"

Addie heard a heartrending wail. It was Dorothy May's voice, but she couldn't see the girl. Panic struck her as she waved her free arm and tried, futilely, to disperse the smoke. She frantically looked about the room. Through the thickening haze she saw a strange glow. And then she saw Dorothy May standing by the kitchen door. Her little white night slip was in flames. The fire leapt up to her face.

"My baby!" Addie screamed. She set Patsy in the middle of the room as she commanded, "Don't move, Patsy!" Then, "Dorothy May, I'm coming for you, baby!"

"Mama!" Dorothy May screamed. "Help me! Help me! Help—"

Addie bolted to the other end of the room and pulled her daughter to the floor. She rolled her on the floor, trying to smother the flames. She could smell the stench of burned flesh and singed hair. She felt nauseous. She could not put out all the flames that engulfed her daughter. Smoke had almost completely filled the room.

"It hurts, Mama. It hurts . . ." Addie heard Dorothy May moan. Then her child was silent.

"Oh, my baby—don't die, Dorothy May. Please, Jesus, please don't let my baby die."

Addie heard loud thuds against the front door. Someone pushed in the door and immediately started coughing. The flames continued to spread throughout the house. "Over there!" Addie shouted to the body. "Get Patsy! She's in the middle of the room here. Get her outta here!"

Addie could barely see the form of a man as he fell to his knees and crawled over to Patsy. He reached out, grabbed her, then dragged the girl out of the house.

Addie was still rolling Dorothy May on the floor. The child was limp. Addie kept rolling. She finally got all the flames out. She picked Dorothy May up in her arms. She could not see through the smoke and did not know where to find the door, but she could feel a gust of air. By instinct, she moved in the right direction and made it out of the house, running into the street. Crowds of people filled the road. She could see their faces clearly because of the brightness of the fire.

Addie turned around; flames were shooting out of the windows. They covered the roof. Everyone stood and watched the spectacle. The roof of the house made a tremendous crash as it caved in. Addie and the girls had made it out just in time.

Addie looked down at Dorothy May and gasped in horror—half of her face, on the right-hand side, was burned and misshapen. Then Addie fainted into a heap on the ground, still clutching her daughter.

"Fire in Colored Town," the newspaper headline read. Then the next line, in smaller type, "House destroyed. Young girl badly burned. Cause of blaze unknown."

"Guess that just 'bout says it," Addie said to no one in particular as she glanced down at the week-old paper folded on a table.

She and the girls had been staying down the street at her parents' house since that night. Patsy was fine. She was out in the yard playing, wearing a neighbor girl's borrowed dress. All Addie could say about Dorothy May was that she was alive.

A white doctor came into Colored Town the night it happened, almost at dawn. That fact spread throughout Clarksville almost as fast as news about the fire. There was a pounding on the front door. Addie's father rushed out of his bedroom, putting on his robe as he strode to the front door.

"Who in heaven's name could it be at this time of night? After all we've been through!" her father said.

Gabe pulled the curtain back and saw a white man with thick gray hair standing on the front porch. The man was still knocking as he opened the door.

"Who is it, Gabe?" Addie's mother called from the bedroom.

"This is the Scott residence. May I help you, sir?"

"I'm Dr. Morgan," he said. And before Gabe Scott could say, "Come in," Dr. Morgan said, "I'm here about the child." He pushed past Gabe to find Dorothy May sprawled on the floor of the front room, Addie on the floor next to her, propped up on one elbow. He went straight to the child and knelt beside her, focused on the burned half of Dorothy May's face. He never took his eyes off the girl as he gave Addie directions to bring him a pot of boiling water, a sheet torn into strips, and a knife.

Later that morning, the doctor said to Addie, "Your daughter came close to losing her right eye. You got to her just in time. Keep her cool and comfortable. She's in a lot of pain now, and it will probably get worse."

He told Addie to expect a big, watery blister. "You won't recognize much of her face for a while, the right side being so badly burned as it is," he warned. "Send someone for me if the blister bursts before I return," he said. He wrote his address on a torn piece of paper and handed it to Addie, and then he left.

Dorothy May slept night and day through most of the next few weeks. When she awoke, she cried, and it was a wail that broke Addie's heart. Addie pulled socks over Dorothy May's hands so that she would not touch the blistered skin on her face while she slept. When the girl's appetite returned, Addie attempted to feed her solid food, but there was too much pain when she tried to open her mouth and chew. Instead, Addie parted Dorothy May's lips slightly with a spoon and fed her chicken broth and pot likker.

Before the blister burst, the doctor returned. "Hold her as tight as you can," he instructed Addie. He leaned in close and burst the blister with a needle and drained it. Dorothy May screamed and thrashed in Addie's arms as the doctor removed the dead skin. Addie looked down at her child: The right side of her face looked hideously red and disfigured. "This will take months, maybe a year, to heal," the doctor said as he left the house. Addie watched as he closed the front door behind him, and then, still holding her scarred child in her arms, she wept.

After Dr. Morgan's visit, Addie could not shake the memory of him peeling the dead skin from Dorothy May's face. And the smell—the smell of the dead skin . . . just the thought of it made Addie feel sick to her stomach. She wanted to leave the house and get the smell out of her nose. She wanted to get her mind off the fire and the burn and her child's face . . . that hideous, misshapen face. The only place she could think to go just then, where there would be nothing to remind her of any of that, was Tom Mitchell's room at the boardinghouse. She had not been to his room at Mrs. Beatty's place for weeks, since before the night of the fire.

"Mama!" Addie called to her mother in the kitchen. "I need some air. I'm going to walk for a spell. Watch my girls for me!"

"Don't stay out long. I can't watch Patsy and take care of Dorothy May all by myself for too long," Laura Scott answered. "Goodness knows, not like I could before the fire."

Not much went through Addie's mind as she walked. It was late afternoon and the heat was stifling, but Addie did not mind. All that mattered was that she was out of the house and didn't have to think about where she was going. Her feet just seemed to know what to do to get her off Franklin Street, out of Colored Town, and over to Mrs. Beatty's place.

When she arrived, she entered through the back door. A girl was in the kitchen ironing by the stove. Mrs. Beatty was nowhere in sight. Addie walked by the parlor where a couple of men were sitting in armchairs, but neither looked up as she walked past and up the stairs.

Addie entered Tom Mitchell's room and looked right away at

his desk, hoping to see him sitting there, hunched over his papers. But the room was empty. Addie looked around the place; she could tell that it had not been cleaned well in quite some time. Instinctively, Addie started doing her usual work, dusting and straightening up. She had started gathering Tom's clothes off the floor and bed and putting them into a basket when he walked in. As glad as she was to see him, when she saw him walk in and close the door, she straightened up and asked, matter-of-factly, "Who's been doin' your shirts?"

But Tom did not hide his joy as he walked across the room, took the basket out of her hands, threw it to the floor, and took her in his arms. "Addie! How long have you been here? I thought I'd have to send word for you to come by," he said. Then he answered her question, "Mrs. Beatty's girl, mostly." He added, "I spend so much time down in Nashville now, it doesn't really matter."

"She doesn't scrub collars," Addie said, talking into his chest.

"It'll do," he said. Then he abruptly ended the small talk and asked anxiously, "How's Dorothy May? I stopped by Dr. Morgan's office the other day. He said burns that bad take a long time to heal. He said he was going to tend to her soon."

Addie started trembling uncontrollably, then burst into tears. "I can't even stand to look at my own daughter's face!" she sobbed. "I had to get out of the house because I can't stand to look at her now!" She described to Tom how the doctor had burst the huge blister and peeled off the dead skin.

"This is the only place I could go," Addie whimpered. "I couldn't think of anywhere else."

"All right, now," Tom said gently. "All right, now." He held Addie while she settled down. Then he took a handkerchief out of his pocket and handed it to her. She blew her nose and wiped her eyes. Then he led her over to the settee and sat down next to her. He gently placed her head against his chest. "Don't worry," he said, stroking her back. "Dorothy will be fine. She'll have whatever she needs to get better. I'll see to it," he assured her. Then he added in a soft voice, "I will always take care of you and the girls, Addie . . . always. Remember that."

Always take care of me and the girls?

Addie almost blurted those words out. Hearing what he said, she felt a rush of blood come to her face. She barely noticed as Tom pulled her closer to him. Hardly heard whatever he was murmuring in her ear. Words Tom Mitchell said to comfort her but got her riled up instead.

Take care of me and my girls? Oh yes, well I can take care of my own self and my girls, fine enough thank you, Mr. Mitchell.

Thoughts rumbled through Addie's head that had nothing to do with Dorothy May and the child's scarred face. Thoughts about how all her life, she had worked. How as a child, her mother had taken her to the tobacco patch to help with the suckering and worming. The tobacco plants towered over her head, so she was not much help with the suckers. But she was good at spotting the worms and pulling them off the broad leaves of the maturing plants. When her mother was not working the fields, she did laundry for a few white families in Clarksville. Addie remembered her mother guiding her small hand up and down the scrub board, teaching her how to work up a lather in the washtub. Then, when Addie was tall and strong enough to steady a hot iron, she quit working the tobacco patch and started doing laundry on her own. She was good with the iron and word spread among some of the white women. That made it easy for her to find work.

Addie lifted her head. She looked over at the laundry basket in the middle of Tom's room. Now she came to Mrs. Beatty's boardinghouse and went straight to Tom Mitchell's room. She did his laundry and kept his room clean. And then she stayed and waited for him because he wanted her there when he came home in the evening. He sent her down to bring up his dinner on a tray. Then she sat with him while he ate. He talked about his day. Sometimes he asked her about the two girls. They talked and even laughed about the goings on in Colored Town and in Clarksville proper. But anytime Addie started to believe that she, a colored woman, had a rightful place with Tom Mitchell, a white man, the envelopes told her something different.

Tom would leave an envelope—addressed to her—on the side of his desk each week. The envelope contained her wages tucked inside. At first, he gave her the same wages Mrs. Beatty would have paid her. Then he added more as the girls were born. Even after the house burned down, when she stayed away to care for Dorothy May, he sent a messenger to deliver the envelope to her. But the envelopes did not contain just her wages. Each envelope reminded her that she really did not belong there with Tom Mitchell. She never would. Even though he was the father of her children and she could not help but think of him when she brushed their long, black, wavy hair in the morning or at night when she kissed their cheeks that were almost as white as his—and no matter what he whispered in her ear as she sat with him those evenings—she would never belong there.

I'm still working to take care of myself, and now my girls, thank you very much, Tom Mitchell. I'm still the woman you summoned back to your room all those years ago. And that's a fact. So yes, I can take very good care of myself and the girls.

Addie pulled away and blew her nose once more. Motioning toward the basket, she said to Tom, "I guess I'll do your shirts, now."

"Leave the shirts this time," he said and pulled her back into his arms.

When Addie returned to her parents' home, later that evening, Willie was there, sitting in a chair in the front room. Addie stood just inside the doorway for a moment and stared at him. Willie had not been around for weeks, not since he'd stormed out of their house the evening of the fire. She had almost resigned herself to the fact that she might not ever see him again. And now he was back. When she finally spoke, her voice was low and cool.

"Where've you been?" she asked. "You're here—at my parents' house—so I guess you've seen our place. What's left of it."

Willie did not answer right away. Then he said, "Your mother acted like she didn't want to let me in the house."

Addie smiled to herself as she imagined her mother standing in the front door, eyeing Willie up and down, deciding whether to let him in the house.

Then he explained, "That night, that night after I left the house, I hitched a ride on a flatbed. Didn't know where it was goin'. Ended up in Nashville. Worked a spell at a warehouse. That didn't turn out too good. Thought I'd come home and try to get hired back at the Shelby farm."

Willie looked around the front room. "Where's Sooner? I didn't see him on the porch ."

"The dog's gone," Addie answered, walking over to the middle of the room.

"What?" he asked, leaning forward in the chair. "Sooner's gone?"

"Ran off sometime after the fire. Or maybe someone took him, I dunno, but he's gone."

Willie slumped back in the chair. "That was my dog," he said. "Did you look for him? Did anyone—"

Addie cut him off and stepped closer toward him. "There was a fire, Willie Jackson, a fire! We lost everything! And you must've heard about Dorothy May . . ." Addie gestured toward the bedroom where Dorothy May slept. "You've been gone who knows where doin' who knows what, so you haven't seen her!" Addie said, her voice suddenly shrill and loud. "Have you even gone over to look at her?"

Willie shook his head and looked down at his hands. "The first thing I heard when I got back to Clarksville and stepped foot into

Colored Town was about the fire, about Dorothy May and the burns on her face."

Then, Addie lowered her voice. "She can't move a muscle in her face without screamin'. She's barely spoken a word since the fire—" She abruptly stopped talking; the memory of that night was back, as if she were hearing the screams, smelling the stench, rolling on the floor with Dorothy May all over again. Coming to at her parents' house, not knowing how she and the girls got there. Cradling Dorothy in her arms. Then, about daybreak, seeing a white man wearing a black coat and carrying a worn black leather bag enter the front room, his gray hair still tousled from having been roused from his sleep. He'd introduced himself and walked straight to where Dorothy May lay on the living room floor.

"Get me a pot of boiling water," he ordered sharply. "Tear a sheet into strips of cloth—wide ones."

"Let me do that," Laura Scott had said, running out of her bedroom and over to where Addie and the doctor knelt on the floor, "I'll take care of the water and the sheets, Dr. Morgan," her mother said to the doctor. "Addie, you stay with the doctor and Dorothy May."

Addie tried to talk to him. "Doctor, I thank God you're here. And I don't know who sent for you, but we've lost everything. I can't pay you now, but I promise . . ."

"Don't worry about the money," he replied tersely. "That's been taken care of."

"What?" And then in her jumble of thoughts she pieced together what had happened.

Tom Mitchell must've sent him . . . News like the fire would have spread outside of Colored Town in no time. He probably made inquiries and found out whose house had burned and . . .

The doctor turned to Addie, then looked to her mother, and spoke deliberately, cutting off Addie's train of thought. "You've got to do as I say and do it right now—I need boiling water, and I need those cloths—"

Willie's voice snapped Addie back to the present. ". . . we'll need someplace else to live."

Still standing, Addie stared down at Willie. She looked at him long and hard. And right at that moment, she did not know if she was glad to see him or no. But it did not matter. There he was.

"This'll do till Dorothy May's stronger. Not gonna move her till her face heals," Addie said.

"I'll be lookin' just the same."

"Do what you want," Addie replied.

"That's all you gotta say?" Willie asked.

There was a long silence between them.

Willie broke the silence. "Well, I guess I picked a bad night to come back home," he said.

"I guess you did," Addie said. She turned and went into the bedroom to check on Dorothy May.

3

1900

SCHOOL BOOKS

A sudden gust of wind blew in, billowing the curtains and scattering across the rug most of the papers Tom Mitchell had been reading. Addie, instinctively, grabbed the corner of the desk and carefully let herself down to the floor. She was due to deliver in the next week or so and reached over her swollen belly to gather up the papers.

"Dorothy May's ten years old, now," Tom said as he took the papers from her hand. "She should be in school with Patsy." He grabbed Addie by the arms and helped her stand back up. "Little Addie is five years old—she'll be in school before Dorothy May if this keeps up," Tom said, looking up at Addie as she stood and leaned against the side of his desk.

He had moved out of Mrs. Beatty's place almost three years earlier and now lived above his office across from the Montgomery County courthouse. The room looked almost identical to his room at the boardinghouse, with a window looking out over the street and just enough space for his settee, bed, desk, and a large armoire.

Addie never mentioned the girls to Tom. She always waited for him to ask about them. He sometimes asked about Patsy or little Addie, who was born just about a year after the fire. But he showed a special concern for Dorothy May and especially her schooling. Addie's thoughts drifted off and she recalled when, right around the time Dorothy turned six years old, Tom had said to her, "You put that girl in school now, so she won't fall behind."

"I've told you how it is with her. She can't go to school," Addie had said. "She has a fit if I try to take her out of the house. She won't even play out in the yard with Patsy." Tears welled up in her eyes. Her voice trembled. "It's that scar! The right side of her face hangs down low. The skin is thick and rubbery . . . she tries to smile but she can't . . ." The tears had streamed down Addie's cheeks. She wiped her nose with her upper arm and kept talking. "She never looks you in the eye. When she has to talk to someone, she looks down at the floor and turns her head so that only the left side of her face shows.

"You've talked to Dr. Morgan," Addie said, glaring down at Tom. "You told me you did! He must've told you how it is with Dorothy May, how she'll probably have to live with that scar for the rest of her life . . ."

"All right, now," Tom had said. "Don't get yourself all worked up."

"She has nightmares," Addie said, almost cutting him off. She stopped for a moment to catch her breath. "The girl screams in her sleep. I run to her and hold her. She grabs her face and screams . . ."

"All right, now. Then maybe she can't start school just yet. But it's not good for her to sit inside all day feeling sorry for herself. She needs to do something to occupy her time." He paused and ran his hand over the top of his head. "I'll inquire before I leave for Nashville. I once overheard Mrs. Beatty talk of a colored woman who works the Henry house. She embroiders their pillowcases, tablecloths, and such. Crochets doilies for the table. I'll make arrangements for her to see Dorothy May and teach her to stitch and crochet. I'll see that Dorothy has a supply of thread and whatever else she needs."

"Ooh!" The sudden kicking of the baby inside her broke Addie's train of thought and brought her back to the present moment. She grabbed her midsection.

"You all right, girl?" Tom asked. Addie nodded. "Come on," he said and pulled her down onto his lap.

"She's taught herself to read," Addie said proudly as she settled in and leaned back against Tom's shoulder.

"Say what? Well, I'll be . . ." Tom said as he rubbed his hand across her belly.

"Wi—," she caught herself. "I, I papered the kitchen walls with pages from the *Leaf-Chronicle*," she explained. "Dorothy stands there—don't know how she does it—she stands there and she can call off words from the paper. Most of the time she gets 'em right, too. Why just the other day, I came into the kitchen and she was readin' out loud 'bout this year's crop of tobacco in the Black Patch," Addie said.

"You get that child in school," Tom said. "She's ready. She'll catch up in no time. I'll arrange to have all of her books and supplies delivered to the house."

Ten years old—can't keep her up in the house forever. But I'm so afraid for that child—how will the other children treat her at school? Will they stare? Will they point at her face and laugh? Will they taunt her until she cries? But no matter, because Tom says Dorothy May will start school now and there's nothing more to say about it.

Tom reached over on his desk and grabbed a framed daguerreotype. Addie knew the image well; she saw it whenever she dusted around his desk. It was a likeness of his grandmother, Louise Thomas. He held it out at arm's length so they both could see it. "You know why I keep my grandmother's likeness on my desk, don't you?"

Tom paused and looked straight down at the picture. Addie knew what was coming next; he had told her the answer before, many a time.

"Because Dorothy May is her spittin' image, bless her heart. And wicked smart, too, just like my grandma."

"I hear you. I'll get her in school," Addie said while she shifted her weight in his lap. She moved his hand and leaned forward. "I better be goin' now," she said. "Help me up."

"My Addie," Tom whispered near her ear. He pulled her closer to him.

"Come on, now," she said.

After a moment, Tom put his hand against her back and helped her stand. Then he led her to the door.

"I'm heading out to Nashville tomorrow, but I'll be back shortly. You send word to me when the baby comes, you hear?"

Addie nodded—looking straight ahead—and opened the door.

"Thank you, kindly," Addie said to the courier after he put the large package wrapped in brown paper and tied with heavy string in her hands and announced, "Delivery for you from McClure's Stationers." She was expecting it after her last conversation with Tom Mitchell: if she knew anything at all about that man after so many years, it was that he was, above all else, a man of his word.

Addie knew the shop. She passed it often on her way to Tom's place across from the courthouse. She sometimes slowed down as she passed—no colored person would dare to enter McClure's—and gazed at the display window as she walked by: gold and silver fountain pens carefully laid out next to bottles of blue and black ink topped with carved crystal plugs. Next to the ink, on a small easel, there was a sign that read "Linen stationery personalized with your initials." When she did stop at the window, Addie could see straight through to a back wall stacked with rows and rows of books. She could scarcely believe she held a delivery from McClure's in her very own hands.

Addie sat at the kitchen table and used a knife to cut the string around the package. She carefully unwrapped the brown paper. Then, she almost gasped.

Good Lord, look at this! Tom Mitchell, what have you sent my baby?

Neatly arranged inside the paper was a stack of primers—one for reading, one for spelling, another for handwriting, and a fourth for arithmetic. The spines of the books looked like some of the ones she'd seen stacked on that back wall at McClure's. There were several composition notebooks, some No. 2 pencils—Addie counted a dozen—and a ruler. There was something else wrapped in more brown paper—no string, just paper folded neatly. She unwrapped the paper to reveal a book bag made of brown canvas fabric with a large brass buckle and a thick web strap. She looked in the folds of the paper to make sure she hadn't missed anything. That's when Addie saw the sealed envelope. She carefully opened it so that she would not tear the paper. She recognized Tom Mitchell's handwriting on the stationery with the initial *M* on the top of the page. The note said, "See that Dorothy May starts school without delay."

Lord have mercy, that man!

"Mama! Mama, what's all this? Is this for me, for school?" Patsy asked, running straight to the stack of supplies and immediately picking up a book. "These are baby books. Are these for little Addie? Is she going to start school?"

"No child," her mother answered. "These are for Dorothy May. Your sister's going to start school presently. Maybe even tomorrow."

"I didn't get new books when I started school! I've never ever gotten new books. Why does Dorothy May get new schoolbooks? Who'd they come from?" Patsy asked, all in one breath.

For the briefest moment, Addie Jackson almost said, "Your father sent these for Dorothy May." Instead, she answered, "There was a note. It just said, 'For Dorothy May's schooling.' And whoever sent this note, well . . . they're right—it's time. Your sister is going to school!"

〰

"Hold your head up, baby," Addie said to Dorothy May as she finished the two braids that hung down the girl's back.

"But I don't want to go to school!" Dorothy May said, twisting in the kitchen chair.

"Now you listen to me—you can't sit around the house stitching and doing needlework your whole life. And you've sat at that front window and watched the children playing up and down the street long enough. Time for you to go to school and be around some of 'em," Addie said to Dorothy May the morning of her first day at school.

"Are they going to laugh at me, Mama?" Dorothy May asked softly, slumping down in her seat.

"No child," Addie said.

"Miss Crenshaw won't let them laugh at you," Patsy added, standing next to her sister. "She'll whack 'em across the hand with her ruler. I've seen her do it!"

"All right, now," Addie said, giving Dorothy May one more hug. "Now you two get going to school." She kissed them both goodbye, then stood on the front porch, leaning against one of the posts as she watched them walk down the sidewalk.

She could see that Dorothy May struggled to keep up with Patsy as she carried her book bag on her left shoulder and her lunch pail in her right hand. Her head was cocked to the side with her cheek leaning against her right shoulder.

How's that child going to see where she's going if she holds her head like that? Addie shook her head. Then she prayed. *Dear Lord, please protect my girls. And especially my dear Dorothy May.*

Addie felt a squeezing pain deep in her belly. She grabbed the post and held it firmly until the pain eased. Then she went back into the house to see about little Addie.

Addie lay in bed under a quilt, curled up on one side. Just as the girls rushed through the front door, home from Dorothy May's first day at school, Addie was gripped by a tight cramp in her belly. She let out a loud moan. Little Addie sat over in a corner of the room in a big rocking chair, playing with her baby doll, and didn't seem to notice. But the two older girls did.

"Is the baby coming?" Dorothy May asked, running into the bedroom.

"Should I go get the midwife?" Patsy asked, coming in behind Dorothy May.

"No, no, no to the both of you," Addie said, trying to speak in as normal a voice as possible as she waited for the pain to pass. The girls stood in the doorway to the bedroom, watching her. Addie shifted her legs under the covers. "Dorothy May, come here and tell me all about your first day at school."

"Well," Dorothy May said as she sat next to her mother, "we walked to school, Mama, and Patsy walks too fast."

Addie glanced over at Patsy and caught the older girl rolling her eyes.

"The teacher's name is Miss Crenshaw. And she's colored, Mama!"

"Is that a fact," Addie said.

"I didn't know she was colored. And she has a long ruler and she hit it across her desk when some of the students didn't pay attention to their lessons."

"What kind of lessons did you have?" Addie asked. She felt another sharp pain. She hoped the girls didn't notice as she grabbed her belly under the quilt.

"First, we did arithmetic, then we had a spelling lesson, and I told Miss Crenshaw that I already knew how to read and she said then I should have no problem with my spelling lessons. And then . . ."

"Then we had recess for lunch," Patsy said.

"Let me tell it!" Dorothy May said.

"But you forgot!"

"No I didn't," Dorothy May said.

"All right, girls," the mother said.

"And at lunch I made a new friend. Her name is Clora."

"Oh, that's so nice," Addie said.

"And we sat under a big oak tree and ate our lunch. And then some boys came by and Clora told them to go away. And they asked me who my daddy was, I guess because they don't know me, and I told them Willie Jackson . . ."

Addie glanced at Patsy. She wanted to see into her eyes, but Patsy was staring down at the floor. Addie had sheltered Dorothy May all those years after the fire. But Patsy had been out and about at church and at school. Now she was twelve years old. Addie knew Patsy would have talked to the older girls.

Girls talk. One of them would have told Patsy the way of things. Lord, she would have heard some of the whispers around church. And if those boys were bold enough to ask Dorothy May about her daddy, then surely there were whispers going around school as well.

Addie willed Patsy to look up so that she could see the truth of it in her eyes. But Patsy kept her head down.

"Mama, are you listening to me?" Dorothy May asked.

"Of course, baby, of course I am," Addie said, directing her attention back to Dorothy May.

"So after lunch we had a handwriting lesson and then reading and then it was time to come home!" Dorothy May said.

"Well I'm so glad you had such a fine day," Addie said. "Both of you."

Addie was relieved: no stares, no snickering. At least, none that Dorothy May had chosen to tell her about.

And even if there had been, what with the way Dorothy May turns her head to the side, she wouldn't have noticed anyway. Just as well for the child's sake.

Addie pulled herself up on one elbow. "Girls, it's time for chores! Now Dorothy May, you go feed those chickens. Little Addie"—the girl looked up—"you help her. And Patsy, you finish up dinner—make some biscuits. I already cooked a pot of collard greens. They're on the stove. I put enough wood in the stove to keep 'em good and hot. Later, when your father comes home, you set out his food, too. Go on now."

With the bedroom door open, Addie could see some of what was going on in the kitchen. She watched as Dorothy May took little Addie by the hand and led her toward the back door, but little Addie broke away and ran under the kitchen table with her doll.

"Little Addie, child, go help your sister," Addie called out. The girl didn't budge from her spot on the floor. Dorothy May went on without her.

It was Dorothy May's job to tend to the chickens. Addie had taught her to put on an apron and fill the pockets with corn feed from a bag on the back porch. Then she was to pick up a cake pan and a spoon that were always kept by the chicken coop gate and lightly tap the back of the pan with the spoon. The gentle tapping sound drew the cock, hens, and baby chicks to her. When they arrived, she'd reach into her pockets, grab a handful of the corn feed, and scatter it from side to side. The birds would peck at the ground, eating the feed.

Addie saw when Dorothy May came back in the kitchen. "Set the table, Dorothy May," she called out.

"Yes, Mama," the girl said.

"And Patsy, set out the pot of greens," Addie said.

Addie lay her head back down on the pillow. She heard a thud as Patsy placed the heavy pot of greens on the kitchen table.

"The blade faces the plate!" Patsy corrected Dorothy May.

"I know how to set the table!" Dorothy May said.

"Mama, Dorothy May's setting the table wrong!"

"I am not!"

Addie pushed herself onto her elbow.

"Lord, Lord, you girls are going to be the death of me! Patsy, let Dorothy May set the table on her own."

"But Mama—"

"No back talk, girl!"

"Yes, Mama . . ." Patsy said quietly.

Addie heard the back door open. She heard Willie's footsteps as he walked through the door.

"Daddy!" Dorothy May greeted him as he walked into the kitchen.

"Hi, Daddy!" Patsy said. "Dinner's ready."

"Set the food out, girls," Willie said.

"The greens and biscuits are on the table already, Daddy," Patsy said.

Addie sat up in bed, clutching the underside of her belly. She could see enough to know that Willie walked over to the small tub of water in the sink to wash his face and hands.

"I started school today, Daddy," Dorothy May said as she and her sisters took their places at the table.

"Um-humph," he said. Addie saw him make his way over to where they sat.

Addie reckoned by now the girls were used to Willie not saying much of anything to either one of them when he came home from work. She had always told them, "Your father's tired. Give him some peace."

But sometimes, anger boiled up inside her. Now she wanted to say, "They can't help how they look! I'm used to you taking your hatred out on me. But can you at least show them a bit of kindness? The child started school today, for Christ's sake!"

But she held her tongue. And Addie watched Willie as he sat down at the table and, without saying a word, reached for the pot of greens.

4

1900

Boy Child

Word spread quickly through Colored Town that Addie Jackson had birthed a baby boy. No one outside of the house had seen the child yet, but at church the Sunday following the birth, the midwife couldn't keep her mouth shut. "That midwife told everything," Deaconess Clark told Addie when she paid a visit, bringing a pot of chicken and dumplings with her. "To a whole circle of women, she said, 'Sister Addie had a rough time of it, birthin' that boy. Breech birth—feet came out first, like this—' then she held her arms out in front of her, mimicking what the baby's legs looked like. Then she said, 'Sister Addie tore real bad, good Lord! I did what I could, but she's gonna be laid up a long time . . . a real long time.'" Mrs. Clark shook her head.

Addie nodded. Nothing much she could do about it. "So now folks know what they know," she said to the deaconess. "But I thank you kindly for bringing over the chicken and dumplings. I'll have one of my girls get your pot back to you right away."

"No rush, Sister Jackson. You just rest up and get yourself healed," the deaconess said as she headed toward the front door. "Don't try to get up; I'll let myself out."

After school each day since the boy was born, Dorothy May sat at Addie's bedside and practiced her handwriting in her notebook while her mother sat up in bed and nursed the baby. Patsy went right to the kitchen and put dinner together, usually eggs fried in bacon grease with green onions or tomatoes from the garden. Sometimes she made biscuits. Little Addie ran between the kitchen and the bedroom, holding her baby doll in her arms.

Addie sent all three girls back to the yard when it was time for her to change her bed. Even after a couple of weeks, the blood was still coming heavy and she did not want the girls to see it. She kept several sheets folded under her, but the blood soaked right through. She could not wash them clean enough; she could see the brown stains as she hung the sheets outside on the clothes-line to dry.

Addie didn't worry about Willie seeing the stained sheets: she barely saw him anymore. He still came home late and left in the early morning. He was a hand at the Shelby farm where they grew 300 acres, more or less, of dark tobacco.

He'd been employed by the Shelby farm when they'd first met at a church picnic. He was sitting over to the side by himself. Addie had never seen him before, but she did notice that he kept to himself. She asked her mother who he was.

"He works the Shelby farm. I've seen him before," Laura Scott told Addie. "Hear tell he walked all the way up from Mississippi, working different farms till he made it here to Clarksville. Don't know why he settled on Clarksville. Keeps to himself like you see there. Nice enough fella."

When the meal was laid out, he filled his plate and sat next to Addie at her table. They talked a bit. Addie could tell he was not much for conversation. She liked that about him. She kept to herself, too, for the most part. He did tell her what she already knew: that he was from Mississippi, and that he worked the Shelby farm. One thing led to another and they started courting. A year later—1886—they were married in a small ceremony in her parents' living room. Her parents were there. So were her brothers and their wives. Her sisters—who had moved to nearby counties after they were married—had come to town and were there with their families. Willie said he didn't have any people that he knew of, so one of Addie's brothers stood as his witness. After the wedding, Addie and Willie moved to a house down the street from her parents' place on Franklin Street.

When the baby boy was just over a month old, Willie looked down at the baby where he lay in his basket. Addie had wondered when he would notice: the child's darker color had started coming in. She watched. She could tell by the movement in his eyes that he saw the little brown hands and the color coming in from his ears and over to his cheeks. She waited for him to say something.

"Well look at that!" Willie finally said. "Lord, Lord, this is *my* boy."

Addie could hear the note of pride in his voice.

Then Willie fell silent. Addie knew what must be going through his head. Coming from Mississippi like he did, he had to know the way of it when the master took one of the colored women as his own. If she was married, the husband knew his place: he would know to stay away from his wife because she belonged to someone else. Willie had known his place. And because of that, he had stayed away from Addie—until he didn't.

"Lord, Addie, you birthed a *colored* baby boy," Willie said.

"Yes, I birthed the boy. But you talk like you had nothing to do with it," Addie said with an edge to her voice.

"Oh my Lord!" he said. Panic suddenly replaced pride in his voice. "Good God—and the judge, he'll know. He'll know it had to be me—that I'm the boy's daddy," he said, his eyes almost bulging out of his head. "So then what? What'll happen to me then?" Willie gripped the side of the baby's basket. For a moment, Addie thought he was going to faint. "Does he know you birthed a colored boy? Have you told him?"

She knew she had to tell Tom Mitchell before he found out on his own.

"No," Addie answered simply.

Addie feared for Willie. As he stood there staring across the room, looking at nothing in particular, she saw the look of fear in his eyes when he asked her, again, "What will he do to me?"

Then Addie's fear suddenly shifted. She pushed herself up and away from her pillow.

Dear Jesus, what have I been thinking? I'm laying here feeling sorry for Willie, wondering what's going to happen to him . . . but whatever Tom Mitchell does to Willie, he could do to me! He could take his pistol out and put a bullet in both our heads. Call out the Order of the Camellia to lynch the two of us—from the same tree. And no one would bat an eye. Heck, colored and white folks would be saying, Got what's coming to them, the both of them.

Addie bent her legs, leaned forward, and rested her forehead against her knees.

And if I'm gone, who's going to take care of my girls and this baby boy? My mother would take the girls, I'm sure of it. And one of my sisters would surely take the baby boy . . .

She lay back down against the pillow. "My babies," she muttered.

Addie looked over at Willie. When they had been married going on two years, and she had not gotten with child, she said to him one morning as they sat in the kitchen before he left for the farm, "Looks like I might be barren."

Willie just grunted. Then he said, "I reckon that's how it is." And he walked out the front door and headed out for the farm.

So when a few months later Addie told him that she was with child, Willie smiled. It was not a big smile—he didn't show any teeth—but the way Willie straightened his back and nodded his head, Addie could tell he was pleased with the news.

When their firstborn, Patsy, was born yellow, Willie didn't say anything. But after the baby's brown color failed to come in, Willie walked over from the basket where he had been looking at the sleeping child and stood over Addie as she shelled peas at the kitchen table.

"That baby's high yellow, pretty much white. Who got to you?" he asked.

Addie was silent. She had been waiting for him to notice, wondered how long it would take for him to see.

"It was one of the fellas at the boardinghouse, wasn't it?" he asked.

Addie kept her head down and kept shelling peas.

Willie slammed his fist down on the table. Addie—startled—knocked over the bowl of peas, sending most of them rolling onto the floor. "Answer me, woman!" Willie yelled.

Addie nodded her head, her eyes on the table.

"Which one?"

"The judge," Addie answered.

"The judge," Willie repeated.

"Judge Mitchell," Addie said.

After that, for the longest time, Willie stayed away from her. He did not so much as hug her or kiss her on the cheek. Addie knew this much: Willie understood how it was. She belonged to a white man now.

Then after a long time, a dozen years in fact, Willie would come home from the field angry about something or another or maybe full of drink, and he would come to her. Afterward, she would reason with herself saying, "What could I do?" Two men laid claim to her. And one was her husband.

But now, Willie looked down at the brown-skinned boy. "What's gonna happen now?" he asked Addie.

"I don't know, Willie. I don't know . . ." she answered.

Willie cleared his throat. "Whatever happens, least now folks'll know I'm still your husband."

He did not look at Addie. He did not smile. He just stared down at the baby boy and nodded his head. "Yep," he said, "now they'll know."

Two days later, Addie stood to the side of the window in Tom Mitchell's room. She had waited as long as she could to come and tell him. She did not want him to hear on his own. He had ways—when they sat in the evenings and talked, he always seemed to know the goings on in Colored Town.

As Tom crossed the street, he looked up at the window. She could not tell by the look on his face if he saw her standing there. She watched him walk up to his office door and enter the building. She listened to his footsteps: he did not stop in his office but started up the stairs straightaway to his room.

His footsteps got louder.

What's going to happen to me and the girls after I tell him? How are we . . .

The door swung open. Her train of thought stopped. Tom looked over to the window and locked eyes with Addie.

"Why'd you stay away so long?" Tom asked as he entered his room and closed the door.

Addie did not answer. She mustered a faint smile.

"I've been laid up in bed. The birthing—"

Tom dropped his leather case on the floor by the settee next to his desk and cut her off. "I missed you, girl," he said, smiling as he pulled her away from the window, bent down, and kissed her forehead. "Why didn't you send word? I had to get the news myself from one of the colored livery boys that you'd had a boy . . ." His voice trailed off. He pulled her closer to him.

"The delivery was hard and long . . . I tore real bad. I'm still not healed," she explained.

"My Addie," he murmured. He held her tight and rocked her in his arms. "When do I get to see my son?"

"Tom Mitchell," Addie said. She stopped. Her heart was pounding so hard she thought it would burst out of her chest. She could barely feel his arms around her. Addie took a deep breath. "The boy's black."

Tom's entire body stiffened as he held her. Then he dropped his arms and let go.

"The baby—" she began. She was going to tell him how the color had just started to come in and she had waited to tell him because, well because . . .

Tom stepped back, raising his arm as though getting ready to slap her.

Addie stopped talking, bracing herself for the blow. Her eyes welled up with tears. But the blow never came. His hand just stayed there, high above his head.

"Addie, Addie—how could you?" he asked, raising his voice.

Addie looked up at his face, but Tom was staring past her, at the space above her head. She could see the rage building up inside of him. His face had turned a fierce red. His whole body started to tremble. After several seconds, he locked eyes with her. She didn't know if he was going to cry out or strike her.

Then the trembling stopped. His hand still raised, he stood stock still. He did not move. Addie was afraid for herself and for Willie, not knowing what Tom might do in a fit of rage.

"He's my husband," she said, trying to explain.

"No!" Tom answered, his voice almost shrill. "*I'm* your husband," he said.

Addie caught her breath. She watched as Tom Mitchell slowly lowered his hand and let it rest on the top of his head. He ran his fingers through his hair. Then he turned around, walked over to his desk, and sat down.

"You betrayed me, Addie," he said, looking down at his desk.

"No, no, no, no, no . . ."

Addie stared at the back of his head, still stunned by what she had just heard. She felt her own rage growing inside of her.

I'm your husband. Yes, she'd heard him say that all right. And it took a strong force of will for her not to shriek, "My husband? You think you're my husband? When, Tom Mitchell, when did you become my husband? When you first told me to come back to your room at Mrs. Beatty's boardinghouse? When you made me wait for you to come home each evening? When I told you I was with child with Patsy? Or maybe it was when Dorothy May was born? Or little Addie? When, Tom Mitchell? When I learned to ignore all of the whispering behind my back as I walked about Colored Town or sat down with my high-yellow girls at church? When in God's name did you become my husband?"

But Addie kept silent and waited for him to speak, trying to calm herself by taking several deep breaths.

Tom Mitchell, hunched over his desk, stared at the framed daguerreotype of his grandmother.

"Dear God, the girls . . ." he whispered.

Addie barely heard the whisper; she leaned forward.

Looking back down at the papers, he said slowly and precisely, and just a bit louder, "I don't ever want to hear word that Dorothy May's been working the tobacco patch. You hear me, girl?" he said.

Addie nodded her head. She could not open her mouth to speak. She did not know what to say.

Reaching over and grabbing the frame, he said, "She looks just like my grandmother, everybody can see that, and I want her to have the respect due a Mitchell. I want her to be the best a colored woman can be. You hear me now? I'll see to it."

Tom paused before adding, "Patsy and little Addie . . . I'll see to them, too . . ." His voice trailed off. He turned in his chair and looked at Addie.

"Folks know you're the mother of my girls. They'll see you with that boy and the whole of Clarksville will know that you betrayed me, Addie." There was a tremor in his voice. "Don't come back here." He turned back toward his desk, this time looking straight ahead.

Addie stood there another moment.

So this is it. This is how it ends . . . He took me in. Now he's letting me go. He's humiliated. Worried about what folks will think.

She knew she had to leave. Heart racing, her breath coming faster, she bolted for the door and left his room, closing the door behind her.

Addie hurried down the steps. Halfway down, she heard a loud thud, as if Tom Mitchell had slammed his fist against the desk. She flinched and stopped mid-step. She listened, thinking he might open the door and call her name. She thought he might come running down the stairs after her and ask her to come back, but there was silence. She continued on down. At the bottom of the stairwell, before she could open the door that led to Tom's office, she was gripped with a sharp pain below her belly. She fell back against the wall.

Addie felt warm and wet between her thighs. She was bleeding again.

And what's going to happen to me now, me and the girls? He says

he'll remember the girls, but will he? And he tells me, don't let Doro-
thy May work the tobacco patch. Well maybe she will and maybe she
won't . . . maybe she'll just have to put down that embroidery hoop of
hers and take in some laundry.

She took a handkerchief from her dress pocket.

"No matter, I'll be fine," she said under her breath. "He can remember the girls or no, the girls and I, we'll be fine. I can take in laundry . . . I can work at the Shelby farm. It's been awhile, but I still know what to do."

She bent over and used the handkerchief to wipe off the blood that flowed down her legs, some of it dripping straight onto the floor. She looked down as she wiped and saw that a small pool of red had collected by her feet. "Damn that blood," she muttered. "Damn that blood."

When she finished wiping herself off, Addie stood up and straightened her clothes. She folded the bloody handkerchief and tucked it inside her bosom. She went through one doorway and then another before she stepped outside. From where she stood on the sidewalk, she grabbed the door and slammed it shut, closing it so hard that the glass pane shook. Addie turned and headed for home.

Addie had just walked out of the kitchen and into the living room when she saw Willie open the front door. Standing there on the porch was an older colored boy. Cap in hand, he delivered his message in a steady voice.

"Willie Jackson?" he asked.

"Yes," Willie answered.

"Judge Mitchell would like to see you this evening. His address is 134 Strawberry Alley. Good day." The messenger boy placed his cap squarely on his head, turned, and hurried down the street.

It had been just under a week since Addie had told Tom Mitchell about the baby boy being black. He had not tried to contact her. But now, he was summoning Willie. Addie felt her chest tighten. Willie had no choice but to go at Tom's bidding, no question about it. He had to answer for what he had done to Addie. He had to answer for the black baby that had come out of her, and Addie knew it. She just didn't know how Tom would handle it.

More colored men than she cared to think about had been lynched because of something or another to do with their wives. She had heard news about such at church and around Colored Town. There was that colored fella, Addie couldn't think of his name right then, whose family lived just outside Clarksville on the border of Montgomery County. His wife did laundry for a white family in a nearby town. Something happened to his wife in that house, and the husband went over there. Said something to the white man. Well, a gang of white men came by the colored fella's house that night. Kicked in his door, dragged him out of his bed . . . They got him all right. They tied a rope around his neck and hung him from a tree.

Willie went into their bedroom. Addie watched him as he took off his dirty clothes and changed into the clean work clothes she had set across a chair for him for the next day.

How did Tom know when to send the messenger? Willie usually worked until late in the evening. How did he know Willie was home early that day? Willie and another fella had gotten into an argument out in the field. The foreman had sent them both home early. Did the judge have someone watching the house?

Willie came out of the bedroom and stood in front of Addie. "If I don't come back," he said, "you be sure and take care of my boy, you hear?"

"Of course, Willie," Addie said. "Of course I will."

Then he walked out of the house.

After Willie left, Addie called the girls in from the backyard where they'd been playing. She sent them down to her parents' place; she figured they'd be safe over there. She decided to keep the baby with her. If a mob showed up at the house that night, they might be less inclined to drag out a woman with a baby still sucking at her breast. Then Addie sat on the living room sofa with the baby boy and waited.

It was still evening and Addie was just about to doze off when Willie Jackson walked through the door.

"Thank the Lord," she said in a low voice.

He walked over by Addie. He didn't sit down next to her. He stood by the sofa and peered straight ahead, not down where she sat. He started talking.

"I got there. Stood outside for a minute. Then I knocked on the door. Judge Mitchell asked me to come in. I looked around his office. No one there but him and me. I looked for a pistol—"

I know where he keeps that pistol. Top drawer, to the left.

"—no whip—nothing. He just sat in a chair next to his desk looking straight at me."

Willie paused. Addie studied his face from where she sat. His jaw was clenched.

"He wants me to be his porter," Willie said.

"Porter?" Addie asked.

"Uh-huh."

"Will he pay you?" she asked.

Addie listened. And when Willie finished talking, she sat there on the sofa, staring down in her lap, working it out in her head. *Tom Mitchell would pay him once each month. Willie would work six days a week. Air out his suit for the next day. Make his bed each day. Change his sheets each week. Keep everything in order. Pick up his meals from Mrs. Beatty's boardinghouse.*

"When do you start?" she asked.

"As soon as I go to his haberdasher. Get fitted for two sets of service clothes."

Addie heard everything Willie had said, but she still did not understand. Why hire the man who fathered her black son?

And then, out of nowhere, it became clear.

First he took me. Now he's taking Willie. It's as simple as that.

"My Lord in heaven," Addie sighed. Then she looked up. Willie was talking.

"You know," Willie said, "five maybe six years before I came up here, I was working down in Mississippi on the old master's land. A colored fella came around on a horse. Called himself a circuit preacher. A preacher of the Gospel he called himself. Said he was preaching the Gospel of freedom. Said we were free to leave that farm. Said the war was over and the slaves were free. Said President Lincoln signed a paper that freed the slaves way before that. He said we could go. We didn't know anything about a war. We knew there was fighting over in the next county, but we didn't know much of anything about it. We did what we'd always done: we worked, we ate, we had a roof over our heads.

"Amos, a big black fella, he said, 'That colored preacher says we can go. I'm leaving.' A few of the others went to the house and told the master. Master ran out and begged us to stay. Amos, he still walked away. I decided to walk, too. After a time, I ended up here."

Willie lowered his voice, almost to a whisper. Addie could barely hear him as he said, "Got a different master now. Name is Judge Mitchell. And you might as well call me his slave!"

5

1912

Dress Shop

"Dorothy May, come on now," Patsy said while she studied the dresses in the window of Mrs. Mayfield's Dress Shop and waited for her sister.

Patsy had always been a fast walker, and Dorothy May was used to her complaints as she, more often than not, scurried to catch up with her.

"I'm right here, Patsy, goodness knows, don't you see me?" Dorothy May said, a little out of breath, as she stepped up next to Patsy.

"Well then look in the window here and look at these dresses. Come on now, look! You're getting ready to go off to that college in Nashville and you're going to need a new dress," Patsy said.

"But I've already sewn some new dresses. Skirts and blouses, too. You've seen me at the sewing machine at home," Dorothy May said.

Dorothy May had applied and been accepted to the very first

graduating class of Tennessee Agricultural and Industrial College, a new school for Negro students. Ever since she received the letter of acceptance, she had been busy sewing clothes and packing her trunk.

"Yes, I saw you and everything you've made is nice enough. But look"—Patsy continued, pointing at a dress in the window— "don't you like the new empire style? And look at that fabric. You can't find fabric like that off the bolt, not in Clarksville."

"It's pretty for sure, but I don't know how that style would look on me," Dorothy May said.

"Then let's go try one on," Patsy said.

"Patsy, what's gotten into you? You know they'd never let a colored woman try on a dress in Mrs. Mayfield's shop," Dorothy May said, looking over at her sister.

"They let *this* colored woman try on dresses," Patsy said, looking into the dress shop.

"You?" Dorothy May asked.

"Yes, me. And you will, too. Come on in," Patsy said, turning her head to look Dorothy May straight in the eye and reaching for her arm.

Dorothy May stepped back. "What are you talking about? I don't want any trouble over a dress. When you asked me to come with you today to go 'window shopping,' I thought you meant for us to walk around the shops in Colored Town. I had no idea—"

"Silly girl! There won't be any trouble. I've been coming in here for a few years, now."

"What?" Dorothy May asked.

"Where do you think I get those nice dresses you see me wearing at the socials and church teas? Hmmm? Where?" Patsy asked.

"Well, I never thought about it. The Emporium, I guess."

"The Emporium. Have mercy, sister, you thought I bought those dresses in Colored Town? Well now I've heard everything," Patsy said, shaking her head.

Dorothy May knew exactly what dresses Patsy was talking about. They were exquisitely tailored. Made with fine fabric.

No one else wore dresses like that, not in Colored Town, that's for sure. But . . . but it's funny that I never asked her about them . . . didn't think I needed to ask, I guess, because I thought I knew: I just assumed she'd shopped at the Emporium like everyone else and bought those dresses there. Maybe put in a special order and had them shipped from out of town. Clerks at the Emporium did that for special customers . . .

Dorothy May looked past the dresses hanging in the window and into the shop. Mrs. Mayfield, the proprietor, was standing behind a counter, looking at them.

"Patsy, she's watching us," Dorothy May said with an urgency in her voice.

"What, who? Oh, Mrs. Mayfield? Don't pay her any mind. But all right, let's just step away from the window for a minute," Patsy said.

Instinctively, Dorothy May looked around to see if anyone else was watching them; she was relieved to see that she and Patsy were the only ones on the sidewalk. She knew that if some white person happened to be walking by and thought they were thinking of doing more than just looking in the window . . . Well, Dorothy May knew there would be trouble no matter what Patsy said.

Patsy took Dorothy May's hand, and they walked several yards down the sidewalk. Mrs. Mayfield's Dress Shop was at the corner of a block of shops that included McClure's Stationers, a florist shop, and a shop that carried fine English bone china. They walked to the end of the block and Patsy led Dorothy May to a small grassy area. They were a few steps away from the china shop.

Patsy lowered her voice and leaned toward Dorothy May as she explained. "A few years ago, right after I got my certificate to teach Sunday school from the Baptist conference, I wanted a new dress—a really nice one—for a tea they were having at church to honor all of the new Sunday school teachers. Do you remember that tea?" she asked her sister.

Dorothy May hesitated before answering. "Well, no, not that I recall."

"No matter. My point is, I wanted a really nice dress—"

"But if you had asked, I could have made you—"

"That's not the point. I know you could have made me a beautiful dress. But I wanted something special. Something I'd never had before. I knew I wouldn't find what I wanted in any of the shops in Colored Town. I don't know what got into me, but I walked over here to Mrs. Mayfield's and went right into her shop."

Dorothy May gasped. "Patsy!" she said. "You could have brought a whole lot of trouble down on our family just over a dress. What made you think—"

Patsy put her finger up close to Dorothy May's lips. "Shhh," she said. "Let me finish."

Dorothy May was stunned, but she stopped talking and listened.

"Mrs. Mayfield was standing behind the counter like just now when we were looking in the window—and the shop was empty. That's why I figured she even let me come into her shop in the first place, because no one was around to see me as I walked in. I started looking at dresses. One dress in particular caught my eye. Mrs. Mayfield had been watching me all the while. I could just feel her eyes on me. Then she walked over to me.

"'Would you like to try on that dress?' she asked me. She had the sweetest tone of voice, as if she really meant it. As if I was really welcome to try on that dress.

"Now I had no intention of trying that dress on. I was just going to buy something that I liked that looked like it would fit and then take it home and maybe have you alter it for me."

Dorothy May just stood there, listening. Not saying a word, not even nodding her head.

Patsy kept talking. "Anyway, I was so shocked, I couldn't say anything. I followed her as she led me to the dressing room. While I was trying on the dress, she brought me a cup of tea and she helped me with the buttons and told me how nice it looked on me . . . and, and then just when I was going to ask her how much the dress was because I was sure it cost more than I had money to pay, she asked, 'Should I put this dress on the account?'"

"What account?" Dorothy May blurted loudly.

"Shhh!" Patsy said.

Dorothy May looked around to see if she had attracted any attention, but no one was coming down the sidewalk, from either direction, anywhere near them.

Patsy continued, "That's what *I* wondered. I sure as anything didn't have an account there. And then it dawned on me—that's why she let me try on the dress. Heck, that woman's no fool. She knows when to cross the color line. That's why she didn't shoo me right out of her shop when I first stepped foot in the door. Because of who our daddy is, she was going to send the bill to—"

"Our daddy?" Dorothy May interrupted. "She was going to send the bill to our daddy?"

Patsy pulled her sister farther away from the china shop.

"Stop playing the fool, Dorothy May," Patsy said, sternly, her voice still low. "You know good and well who I'm talking about."

"What do you mean? Who are you talking about?" she asked.

Daddy—a colored man—would never have been allowed to have an account at Mrs. Mayfield's dress shop. Never. And Lord knows he didn't make the kind of money to buy any of us girls, or even Mama, a dress there anyway.

And then, out of nowhere, something else came to mind, something she hadn't thought about in a good long while:

Those boys at school, the ones who ran by at recess asking me, Who's your daddy? Or while I was sitting at my desk finishing my lessons, one of them would walk by, lean over and whisper, Who's your daddy? I thought they were being silly, just acting like boys do sometimes.

"All right, little woman, play the fool all you want! But I'm talking about Judge Mitchell, our real father—Judge Tom Mitchell," Patsy said.

"What?" Dorothy's mouth fell open. She was dumbstruck. "Patsy you have surely lost your mind. Our father is Willie Jackson, our mother is Addie Jackson. What in heaven's name are you talking about our 'real' father?"

Patsy grabbed Dorothy May's other hand and turned it over. She jabbed her finger into the skin. "Look at your skin. You didn't get this high-yellow color from Willie Jackson, that's for sure. Judge Mitchell, girl, that white man gave you this color—just not his name!"

"What? Our daddy's just his porter," Dorothy May said.

"And Mama was his housekeeper. She went over there every day until our brother, Willie boy, was born. I always figured it was too much for the judge, Willie boy being black and all like Daddy . . . So that's when Mama stopped going over there and Daddy started working as his porter."

Patsy stopped talking and casually glanced around as the door to the china shop opened and shut. An older white woman walked by them, not seeming to notice that they were even standing there.

Patsy stepped closer to Dorothy May and started up again. "He's always had a soft spot for you. Always fancied you all these years. Sending you packets of school supplies—from McClure's Stationers, no less! Boxes of embroidery thread would appear on our doorstep . . . I knew who those things came from. It bothered me at first. But then I understood. I have eyes just like everyone else. Look in the mirror, Dorothy May—it's because you're the spitting image of Louise Thomas, the wife of that old Confederate senator, Gustavus Thomas. Louise Thomas is Judge Mitchell's grandmother, his mother's mother. To this day, it must drive that old Thomas woman crazy to see you out and about around town. Everybody who has eyes to see can look at you and tell that."

Dorothy May was stunned. Her knees felt weak. She moved over a couple of steps and held her left arm out to steady herself against the brick wall of the china shop. She was listening to Patsy, but she was thinking to herself as well.

I never thought it through. For so many years after the fire and the burn—

At the thought of the fire, Dorothy May instinctively raised her right hand and placed it against her right cheek.

I didn't leave the house. And when I did leave it was because I started school. I never asked Mama why the schoolbooks and supplies came every year or even who sent them. And before I started school, I learned to do needlework. I never asked who sent over that old colored woman to teach me to embroider and crochet before I was healed enough to start school. It was him all those years.

Patsy took her index finger and jabbed it at Dorothy May. "And who do you think sent you that treadle sewing machine a couple of years ago so that you could make more of those dresses you wear? You know you were the first person to have one of those things in their house in the whole town of Clarksville. No one in Colored Town, not even a white person in all of Clarksville, had one before you did. I watched you read that instruction book, teaching yourself to use that thing, wondering what the white folks in town would think once word got out that you didn't have to sew by hand like all the other women in town, that you had a machine to do it for you."

Dorothy May felt her face flush red, embarrassed for never having thought through what made her life different from the lives of most other Negroes in Colored Town. Dorothy May looked down at the back of her hand. She could feel where Patsy had jabbed her skin.

And the color? I just thought Patsy and little Addie and I are bright. Willie boy's dark. It all seemed to make sense. Growing up, we weren't the only family like that. There were other children who were bright-skinned and who had brown-skinned parents. I just figured that's how some colored families are.

She looked over at Patsy who stood there staring at her and asked, slowly, "But how did you know? Who told you?"

"Dear child," Patsy said. She leaned in closer and talked right up in Dorothy May's face, "Either you recognize the ways of the world or you don't. White folks cross the color line when it suits them. No one had to tell me. Judge Mitchell took a fancy to Mama, his housekeeper, and she's got three girls to prove it. You think Mama's gonna tell me? You think Daddy's gonna tell me? Some things you just look at and figure out for yourself."

Patsy went silent.

Dorothy May looked down at the ground and shook her head.

Those times that I was sitting on the porch at home or at Grandma-Grandpa Scott's house. I'd be sitting there doing my embroidery or crocheting a pillowcase and women, colored neighbors, would walk by and say things just loud enough that I could hear them. Things like, Um-hum, look at that girl, sitting on the porch stitching. Addie raises them gals to think they're white girls. Too good for the tobacco patch . . . I heard that talk, but I didn't think anything of it because folks are always going to talk about something. Mama always said that. Just ignore ignorant talk, she always said to me. And now, now I'm going away to that new colored college. Not the tobacco patch but the college, to study to be a teacher . . .

"And who do you think is going to pay for you to attend that new college for Negroes over in Nashville, that Tennessee Agricultural and Industrial College?" Patsy paused, slightly out of breath from talking fast, and put her hand on Dorothy May's shoulder. "Answer me that, girl. Who?"

"In the acceptance letter, they said I had a fellowship . . ." Dorothy May trailed off.

Of course. The judge is providing the fellowship.

"Listen to me. I don't deny that you deserve what he's done for you. I never was much inclined toward school. I was ready to start courting as soon as I went as far as I could go over at the schoolhouse. And I've got the feeling that I've been courting long enough now. Don't want to be a spinster. Harry Moore has been coming around longer than any of the others. He'll be good enough, I suppose. Daddy likes him. Mama doesn't much care for him. But, no matter—what I'm trying to say is, you're as smart as a whip. He picked you. You're going to that college, and I'd be willing to bet good money that you're going to come back to Clarksville and be the teacher at the colored school. You'll be looked up to in Colored Town. You'll be the one who sits at the head table with the pastor and the pastor's wife, and people will walk up and greet you and smile. The men will tip their hats and the women will curtsy. He picked you for that life. You need to know that—he picked you!"

Dorothy May was breathing heavy. She was still trying to understand her family, her life, her mother working for the judge, and then her father working as his porter.

"You said that after our brother was born, Mama stopped working as his housekeeper and that's when Daddy started working as his porter. When he started working for him, Daddy knew Judge Mitchell was our father?"

When she was younger, Dorothy May didn't really spend much time thinking about where her mama and daddy worked. She knew that Mama did housekeeping in town and Daddy worked the tobacco patch, until he didn't. But exactly when he started working as a porter, wearing different clothes to work . . . when she was young, she didn't think a thing of it. It was later that she found out that he was Judge Mitchell's porter.

"Patsy," Dorothy May asked again, "he knew? Daddy knew about the judge and Mama?"

Before Patsy could say another word, Dorothy May answered herself.

Of course he knew! That would explain so many things: Why he was so cold and distant toward me and Patsy and little Addie. Why he would come home sometimes and not even look at us. Mama would say it was because he had worked hard all day and he was tired, but something didn't feel right about that. No matter how tired, a little kindness to your own children . . .

"Of course he knew," Patsy said, breaking into Dorothy May's thought. "And that's their business. That's all I can say. It's their business."

There was a silence between Patsy and Dorothy May, a long silence.

Dorothy May's breathing began to slow down. She fiddled with her skirt. Too many thoughts, questions whirred through her head.

So, I'm a Mitchell? From the Thomas line? The Thomas family, esteemed across the entire state of Tennessee. I learned about Gustavus Thomas in school: he was a senator for the Confederacy for the state of Tennessee. To hear Patsy tell it, that's my great-grandfather. I'm from that bloodline. And people knew? People could look at me and see that Louise Thomas—the woman who walks around Clarksville like royalty because she's the wife of Gustavus Thomas—is my great-grandmother? How could I have been so blind to what was going on in my own family? I feel like an absolute fool!

Patsy touched her sister's arm. "Dorothy May?"

Dorothy looked up, still deep in thought.

"Listen to me," Patsy said. "Now I go to Mrs. Mayfield's shop and when I see a dress that I like, I put it on Judge Mitchell's account. The judge pays for my dresses. He does that much for me. You, dear sister, are going away to college. He's paying for that. And today, you're going to go into Mrs. Mayfield's shop and you're going to pick out for yourself the nicest dress you can find to wear at that school for when you have socials with your new friends and teas with the dean. You hear me, sister? You and I and little Addie, we're just as much a part of the Thomas Mitchell clan as the whole lot of them over on Cumberland Hill. Even Mrs. Mayfield knows that!" Patsy said. "You hear what I say?"

Dorothy May did not respond right away.

She looked over at her sister and took a deep breath. Then she nodded. "I hear you." Patsy took her by the hand, and they walked back down the sidewalk until they were just outside of McClure's Stationer. Dorothy May stopped and pulled Patsy close to her side. She whispered in her sister's ear, "Does little Addie know?"

Patsy smiled and answered, "If she doesn't already, she'll figure it out soon enough." Then she squeezed Dorothy May's hand and said, "Either way, sooner than you did, I suspect!"

They both entered Mrs. Mayfield's Dress Shop.

"Well, good afternoon, Miss Jackson," Mrs. Dora Mayfield said to Patsy. "It's been quite some time since I've seen you. And I see you've brought your sister. Good afternoon to you, too, Miss Jackson. Are you looking for anything in particular? I noticed you admiring that empire-waist dress hanging in the window."

"Mrs. Mayfield, my sister is preparing to leave for college. She'll be a student in Nashville at Tennessee Agricultural and Industrial College."

"Oh, your family must be so proud of you, young lady," Dora said to Dorothy May, nodding her head and smiling.

"Thank you, ma'am," Dorothy May answered tentatively. She looked over her shoulder at the door to see if anyone was coming in after them. Maybe someone had seen them enter and was coming in to see what these two colored girls were doing in Mrs. Mayfield's shop. But no one else came in.

"Well then, we must see you off properly," Dora said. "I have just the dress for you. I've kept it in the back, waiting for the right customer, but I think it would suit you perfectly."

Patsy nodded at Dorothy May. Dorothy May followed Mrs. Mayfield with her eyes as the woman parted a curtain and went into the back room. She returned quickly with a dress draped across both of her arms.

"This fabric, my dear, was imported from Europe. The dress was made in New York City by expert seamstresses. All of the smartly dressed young ladies will be wearing this style, I assure you. Come"—she motioned with her head—"let's get you into the fitting room. I don't think this will need much alteration, not at all. My girl will have this ready for you before you head on off to college. I'll have her deliver it right to your house."

Dora disappeared behind the curtain. Patsy followed close behind her.

Dorothy May stood in the middle of the store and looked around.

Good God, did everyone in town know about my lineage but me?

"It appears so," she murmured quietly, answering her own question.

"Dorothy May, come on," Patsy whispered as she stepped back out onto the shop floor. Then she held out her hand and beckoned her in. Dorothy May followed Patsy into the fitting room.

6

1912

DEATH NOTICE

Dorothy May stood in the doorway of her dormitory room as she opened the envelope and read the short, handwritten message: "Sister, I thought you should know. It was probably posted in the Nashville newspaper as well. Love, Patsy." Folded inside the notepaper was a clipping from the Clarksville newspaper. Dorothy May unfolded the clipping: it was a death notice.

Thomas Mitchell Passes on to His Reward—We regret to announce the death on October 31, 1912 of Thomas Mitchell, a son of the late George Mitchell and a grandson of the esteemed Confederate Senator Gustavus Thomas . . . At a young age, he became a member of the Tennessee bar and distinguished himself by being elected attorney general of the state of Tennessee in 1894 at the age of twenty-six, the youngest on record . . . He was considered a generous and kind-hearted gentleman. He was unmarried, and his nearest relatives surviving him are two sisters and four brothers. The funeral will be held tomorrow . . .

Dorothy May closed the door to her room, then she walked

over and sat down on her bed. Her chest felt heavy. She reread the following line from the obituary over and over: ". . . his nearest relatives surviving him are two sisters and four brothers . . ."

So this is how it is. I've got two fathers: one white and one colored. The white one never acknowledged me in public, the colored one never acknowledged me in private—except once.

It had been right before she'd left for the train that would take her to college.

"Daughter, you do our race proud. You do your mother and me proud," Willie Jackson said as he and Addie stood with Dorothy May on their front porch, waiting for the livery boy to take her and her trunk to the train station. He kissed her forehead. Dorothy May felt her cheeks flush red, and not because he had kissed her. No, she knew right away what felt different about that moment: it was neither the farewell nor the kiss but the fact that after all those years of living under the same roof, she had never before heard him refer to her as his daughter.

"He called me daughter," she said out loud in her room, then smiled and shook her head. "At the age of twenty-two and about to go off to college he finally—"

The sound of the dinner bell startled her and broke her train of thought.

"Oh," she said as she heard the other young women leaving their rooms and hurrying down the stairs to the dining hall. She sat on her bed a while longer, holding the letter, listening to the footsteps outside her door.

There was a knock on her door. "Dorothy May? Are you coming?" It was Hazel Johnson, one of her tablemates.

"Yes, yes I'm coming," she answered. As she walked over to her dresser, she put the note and the clipping in the envelope and placed it next to her hairbrush. She looked in the mirror.

"Lord, I look like I've seen a ghost," she said. She put a little rouge on her cheeks and tidied her hair before she left her room.

When she arrived in the dining hall, she was the last one to be seated at her table. Hazel, Arthurine Lawrence, Sarah Brown, Maddie Williams, and Mary Jean Clark were already seated. They were assigned to table number nine, out of the ten tables arranged throughout the room.

The bell rang a second time, just as Dorothy May sat down.

"If you had been late, our whole table would've all gotten a demerit, you know that," Hazel leaned over and whispered to her. "What took you so long?"

Dorothy May knew that neither Hazel nor the other students at the table wanted to jeopardize their good standing at the college. They realized their good fortune. They and the other young women in the dining hall—the young men were housed in the dormitory next door—represented the inaugural class enrolled in Tennessee Agricultural and Industrial College, Tennessee's first state college for Negroes. They came from across the state, and they represented every class and background of Negro. Some of their families owned small businesses—barbershops, repair shops, dress shops, and the like. Maddie Williams's family owned a funeral home in Memphis and was considered wealthy. Other families worked the tobacco fields. Some of their mothers took in laundry. Other students were from families where one of the parents had been educated in the North as a teacher or minister. But no matter the background, they were honored to be part of this new college that would help ensure the progress of the Negro race in the state. The college's primary mission was to train an ongoing supply of teachers for the colored children in the Tennessee public schools.

Before Dorothy May could respond, a hush came over the dining hall as the housemother, Mrs. Wilson, stood at the head of the room and said grace. She was a deep-brown-skinned woman who wore her hair pulled tightly into a bun at the back of her head. With her straight back and square shoulders, she looked composed and regal as she bowed her head.

When Mrs. Wilson sat down, the young women passed around the platters of food according to the dining room protocol: first the meat plate, then the vegetable dish followed by rice or potatoes. Some days, before the main course, a hot tureen of soup was placed in the center of the table, and one student would serve and pass the bowls to the others at her table.

Once everyone was served at her table, Dorothy May began eating. She looked forward to the late-afternoon meals. They reminded her of meals at her grandparents' house or at home with her mother and sisters. Not that the food tasted nearly as good: it was plain for sure. It was the feeling of family that she treasured and that the rituals in the dining hall gave her. The girls could have been her cousins; they were all close in age, though Dorothy May never let on that she was a few years older than they were because of the years she had stayed home and out of school after the fire. And one, Hazel Johnson, even had a skin color as bright as hers.

Almost as soon as Dorothy May put her fork to her mouth, Maddie called her name. "Dorothy May, you're so good at math, what did you think of that algebra exam this morning? Was it a tough one or not? What did you think? Because I thought it was one of the hardest exams we've had since we've been here?" she asked her.

Dorothy May pointed toward her mouth as she finished chewing. Then, as she answered, she instinctively leaned her right cheek slightly toward her shoulder as she looked across the table at Maddie. While much of her right cheek had smoothed out from the thick, rubbery skin she had when she was a younger girl, a scar still remained and her cheek still hung a bit. She often found herself reverting to her habit of trying to hide that side of her face. Realizing what she was doing, she straightened her head and answered.

"It was a tough one," Dorothy May said, "but nothing that Professor Mays hadn't already covered."

"Well I don't recall him covering half of the equations that were on the test," Maddie said. "I don't think it's fair for him to test us on work we haven't covered in class." Dorothy knew that Maddie had helped her father keep the accounting books for their funeral home in Memphis. Dorothy also knew that Maddie prided herself on being quick with math and calculations.

"I studied from my notes," Dorothy May said, "and everything on that test was in my notes."

"Well I don't see how I could have missed so much from my notes," Maddie said. "Mary Jean, what do you think?" Maddie asked. "Were those equations in your notes?"

As Mary Jean answered, Dorothy felt a hand on her shoulder. She looked over and saw Mrs. Wilson, the housemother, standing behind her.

Mrs. Wilson whispered in her ear, "Dorothy May, dear, may I speak with you for a moment?"

Dorothy May followed her out of the dining room. They stood to the side, out of the view of the others in the room.

"I just received a note from Dean Conrad's office. The dean would like to see you in his office after the dinner hour."

"Yes, ma'am. Thank you, Mrs. Wilson," Dorothy May answered.

"Finish your meal, of course, but then hurry over to his office."

"Yes, ma'am."

Dorothy May waited a moment to compose herself. As she walked back to the table, she tried to put a smile on her face, but inside she was shaken.

"What was that all about?" Sarah asked as Dorothy May sat down.

"Oh, she was just saying there was a change in my duties at Sunday's tea."

"Well, she could have just told you that at the table without interrupting your dinner," Mary Jean said.

"What are you ladies wearing to the tea?" Arthurine asked.

Dorothy May did not join in the conversation about the tea and dresses, because she did not expect to be at the tea on Sunday.

If she were going, she would have worn the dress from Mrs. May-field's Dress Shop. And it would have been, she had no doubt, the finest dress worn at the tea. Now something else was on her mind. She was sure the dean wanted to see her because he had seen Tom Mitchell's obituary in the Nashville paper, him being a former state attorney general and all. He would tell her that because of Judge Mitchell's death, the fellowship that covered her tuition and fees would no longer be forthcoming, and she would have to leave the college if she had no other means of payment. She looked around the table as her friends chatted about their dresses and the tea. They had grown close over the first few weeks of class, sitting together at their assigned table at each evening meal, chatting about classes and families and who was who among the young men in the dormitory next door. She would miss them when she returned to Clarksville.

She hurried and finished her meal. As she rose to leave the table, Maddie looked up and said, "Where are you going, Dorothy May? You know Mrs. Wilson doesn't like us to leave the dining hall until everyone has finished their meal. And you didn't tell us what you're wearing to the tea."

"I don't think she'll mind. I have some business to take care of," Dorothy May answered. "I'll show you—all of you—my dress later." Trying not to look worried, she took her plate to the bussing cart.

Dorothy May walked across the courtyard to the administration building. The dean's office was on the first floor, and his secretary was still at her desk. Dorothy May entered the vestibule where the secretary sat.

"I'm Dorothy May Jackson. I received word that Dean Conrad would like to see me."

"Yes," she said, looking up at Dorothy May, "Dean Conrad is expecting you. You may go right in."

"Thank you," Dorothy May said. She knocked on the door.

"Come in."

When Dorothy May entered the dean's office, he walked around from behind his desk and greeted her with a handshake. She had seen him from the stage at the welcoming assembly and from across the courtyard as she made her way to classes, but this was the first time she had been face-to-face with him. He was a short man, not much taller than she, and his skin color was a darker brown than it appeared from a distance.

"Please, have a seat," he said, gesturing to one of the chairs opposite his desk.

He returned to his chair.

She cleared her throat. Her palms were moist.

"Miss Jackson," Dean Conrad began, "may I begin by saying that I was recently made aware of the death of your . . ." The dean paused. "Your patron," he continued. "Your patron, the Honorable Thomas Mitchell. And I am deeply sorry for your loss."

"Thank you, Dean Conrad," she said, wiping her hands against her skirt.

Patron, you call the judge? My patron—that's the word you chose? You might as well have called him my father. You know, oh yes, I'm sure of it. You know the judge is my father. Well, then, let's get on with it.

The dean continued, "Judge Mitchell was one of the early and most generous contributors to this college when the founders of the school were seeking donations to begin constructing the facilities and hiring teachers. Judge Mitchell made a very clear stipulation that he would make a substantial donation but that a portion of the money must first and foremost be set aside to fund the education, as well as the room, board, and a small stipend, of one Miss Dorothy May Jackson."

The dean nodded toward Dorothy.

"Your place in this college is secure for as long as you remain a student in good standing, Miss Jackson," he said. "Again, I am sorry for your loss."

Dean Conrad stood up, the signal to Dorothy May that she should do the same.

"Thank you kindly, Dean Conrad," Dorothy May said as she stood by her seat. "And good evening."

She extended her arm. The dean reached across his desk and shook her hand.

As Dorothy May left the administration building and walked across the courtyard, she felt as if she were walking on air—the heavy burden she had been carrying since she opened the envelope just a few hours earlier had been lifted. She would stay at the college. She would be with her friends. She would finish her education and become a teacher. She headed toward the park across the street from the campus.

He provided for me. He took care of me, just like Patsy said.

She smiled as she sat down on one of the benches in the park.

The obituary was wrong. It should have read, "He is survived by three daughters: Patsy, Dorothy May, and Addie. Dorothy May is a student at Tennessee Agricultural and Industrial College in Nashville where she will complete her studies at the Teachers College."

Dorothy May was shaken out of her daydream by a harsh sound. She looked up, startled, and saw the face of an older white man. He was wearing a policeman's uniform. The sound was his nightstick hitting the back of the bench.

"Gal, no coloreds are allowed to sit on these benches in this park. You get a move on," he said, and then hit the tip of her shoe with his nightstick. "Go on, now!"

"Yes, sir," Dorothy May said, looking toward his face but not making eye contact. She quickly got up from the bench and turned away from the officer, crossed the street, and returned to campus.

When she got back to her room, she sat at her desk and wrote a letter to her mother. She explained in the note just what Dean Conrad had said and how the judge had provided for her education, even in death.

"Merry Christmas, Dorothy May!" little Addie squealed in excitement.

"Welcome home!" Patsy said.

Patsy, little Addie, and their mother all rushed to greet Dorothy May when she opened the front door. She had completed her first semester at Tennessee A&I.

"Give me a hug, give me a kiss! How was the train ride?" her mother said. "Merry Christmas, baby!"

"I went shopping in Nashville and brought home some Christmas presents," Dorothy May said after she hugged her mother and sisters. She pulled some small boxes wrapped in red paper out of her duffel bag. "Here, I'll put them on the table next to the gingerbread." She grabbed a square of the cake. "I could smell the gingerbread as soon as I walked in the door. I knew I was in the right place. Who did the baking?"

Their mother nodded toward Patsy. "Patsy's been doing most of the cooking around here, lately. Getting ready to marry Harry Moore, right girl?"

"Really, Patsy, really? When's the wedding?" Dorothy May asked.

"Next spring, probably," Patsy said.

"Oh, Patsy, I'm so happy for you!" Dorothy May said. "But why didn't you write to me and tell me?"

"I wanted to tell you myself, in person. But it looks like Mama beat me to it!" Patsy said, glancing over at her mother and grinning.

"Oh, that's all right," Dorothy May said. "We can talk, and I can help you make plans while I'm home these next few weeks!"

Then Dorothy May looked around the living room.

"Where's Daddy? Is he working somewhere else now?" Dorothy May asked. "And where's Willie boy?"

"Willie boy's down the street playing stickball with some neighbor fellas. Your father, he's at the lawyer's office," her mother said.

"Lawyer? What lawyer? What's wrong?" Dorothy May asked.

"Nothing's wrong, baby, so don't worry," Addie said. "They're reading the judge's will—Tom Mitchell's. Your father got an invitation to the reading."

"Does that mean the judge left him some money?" Dorothy May asked. "The lawyer wouldn't invite him if the judge didn't leave Daddy something."

"We'll see, baby. We'll see soon enough," her mother said.

"You should have seen Daddy," little Addie said. "He was wearing his work clothes—his porter suit—when he left. It was just like the judge was still alive, waiting for him and all."

"Is that a fact?" Dorothy May said.

"All right girls, enough talk about your daddy and that will," Addie said. "Patsy, why don't you go on into the kitchen and get dinner started. Remind Dorothy May what real home cookin' tastes like. I'm sure she's had enough of those dining hall meals they've been serving over at that college," Addie said as she put her hands on Patsy's shoulders and turned her around to face the kitchen doorway.

While Patsy started dinner, Dorothy May took her duffle bag into the bedroom she shared with Patsy and little Addie. Dorothy May shook her head as she unpacked her things and placed them in a dresser drawer.

Daddy worked so hard for that man. So many times after supper, leaving to go back to the judge's rooms, even on Sundays, his day off. Going to finish up a little more work for the judge, he would say as he headed out the door. Just going to polish up his shoes before he goes to

Nashville, or, he's coming in late tonight, I'll just be there to take his things and air them out for tomorrow.

Willie Jackson explained to the girls, many a time, why he did all that extra work for the judge. He told them, "He's going to remember me in his will. He said that, yes he did. 'Willie,' he'd say, 'you've done good work all these years. You've worked hard, and I won't forget it. I won't forget everything you've done for me. I'm going to remember you in my will.'"

Dorothy didn't know if he was repeating what Tom Mitchell told him or no. But later that day, when Willie Jackson came home from the lawyer's office, she figured they would know for sure, one way or the other. "That's the least the judge could do," she muttered in a low voice, "after Daddy raised us girls and kept a roof over our heads. Leaving him something in that will is the least the judge could do."

"Merry Christmas, Daddy!" Dorothy May said from where she sat on the living room sofa, looking up from her needlework. When he walked in the house, she could see a look of disappointment on his face.

He smiled weakly. "Welcome home, girl!" he said. He walked over to the table where Dorothy May had piled the gifts and picked up a piece of gingerbread.

Addie came out of the kitchen, and Patsy and little Addie followed behind her.

"So how did the reading of the will go?" Addie asked him.

"Yes, Daddy, how'd it go?" Patsy and little Addie both asked.

Willie shook his head. He sat down on the sofa and finished his cake.

Then he spoke. "That lawyer's office was full of white folks. I was the only colored there," Willie said. "The lawyer commenced to read what he called the Last Will and Testament of Thomas Mitchell. He read off a lot of names and who got what and how much they got before he read off my name."

"C'mon, tell us—how much did he leave you, Willie?" Addie asked.

"Then he gets to me," Willie said. "'I leave to Willie Jackson,' the lawyer read, 'the sum of two hundred and fifty dollars.'"

Patsy gasped. Little Addie placed her hand over her mouth.

Dorothy May dropped her needlework in her lap. She was stunned.

Two hundred and fifty dollars? That's what he left Daddy? This was the man who gave money to help start the Negro college. Who made arrangements to pay for my tuition and room and board for as long as I remain a student at that school. Oh my Lord!

Dorothy May glanced over at her father. He was looking down at the floor. He took a deep breath. "You all heard right," he said, shaking his head and sounding tired, "$250."

"All the work I did for that judge . . . all those years . . . I worked for him a dozen years and that's what he left me," Willie said.

"But he told me . . ." Addie started to say. Then she stopped.

Dorothy May looked over at her mother, waiting to hear the rest of what she had to say.

What did he tell you, Mama?

But she knew better than to ask that question out loud. This conversation was now between her mother and Willie. Dorothy May just listened. The other girls were silent as well.

"Yes, Addie, what did he tell you?" Willie asked, staring over at Addie with an edge to his voice. "What did the man say? Because I know what he said to me, too, Addie. 'Willie, I'll remember you in my will. Willie, I'll remember everything you did for me.' And the man just spoke to me through the grave, in front of a room full of white folks, Addie, and he spoke loud and clear. '$250,' he told me!"

Dorothy May watched as her mother turned and walked toward the kitchen.

"It's just that I never would have thought that of him. Never," Addie said as she left the room.

"Well, now you know better, Addie, don't you?" Willie called after her.

Dorothy May heard the back door open and shut. Then she turned toward Willie.

He looked over at the face of each of the girls. "Now you all know better."

7

1922

COURTSHIP

Dorothy May had been the teacher at the Clarksville Colored School for six years. Since her first day back at Clarksville, the school board had contracted for her to have a room in Mrs. Shelby's boardinghouse. Mrs. Shelby was a widow, an elderly colored woman, and well-off by any standard. Her husband had been a seaman, one of the free Negroes who worked the merchant ships that sailed along the eastern coast of the United States. He died during a storm at sea. Mrs. Shelby took his death pension and purchased the largest house in Colored Town, a huge Victorian home. She opened a boardinghouse and it soon became the place where all of the visiting colored politicians and elected officials, as well as pastors and their wives, stayed when they came through Clarksville and Montgomery County.

Mrs. Shelby was thrilled to have Dorothy May as a permanent tenant. There were other long-term boarders, but most were elderly gentlemen of no note. Mrs. Shelby extended Dorothy May every courtesy, from having the housekeeper empty the commode in her room each day to serving her breakfast out on the veranda on hot summer mornings. "My esteemed teacher," Mrs. Shelby called Dorothy May when she introduced her at her Sunday afternoon teas.

When she first returned to Clarksville, Dorothy May would sometimes accompany the young people from Mt. Zion Baptist Church as they picnicked and collected nuts that had fallen from the hickory and walnut trees along the Cumberland River. Dorothy May enjoyed going "nutting," as they called it, in the cool of the evening. After those early years, she considered herself too old to join the young people, and she stayed mostly to herself at Mrs. Shelby's place. She had her needlework to keep her busy. She prepared lessons during the school year. She posted letters to her college friends. Hazel and Maddie posted return letters quickly. Maddie had returned to Memphis, teaching at a colored school there until she married Roy, just as she said she would, and they started a family. Hazel stayed in Nashville and was working in the dean's office at the college.

"I don't seem to fit in anywhere," Dorothy May confided in a letter she wrote to Maddie. Without letting her friend know that she was, at the time she penned the letter, thirty years old, she wrote, "I'm too old to socialize with the young people at church. And I don't fit in with the women who are married with young children. So, I just try to be the best teacher I can be. I am making the most of this opportunity that is not offered to many, just as you, Mary Jean, and Sarah told me six years ago when we sat together in the dining hall and I read aloud the letter from the superintendent of the Clarksville schools."

m

Dorothy May Jackson stood at the window in her dormitory room to catch more of the afternoon sunlight as she read the letter.

"Dear Miss Jackson: Miss Crenshaw, the teacher at the Clarksville Colored School, has resigned her position in order to care for her ailing mother. We would like to offer you, an esteemed daughter of Clarksville, the position. Please reply to this offer by return post as soon as possible to let us know."

Dorothy May folded the letter but held it in her hand. Her beloved teacher from so many years back was leaving the school.

What do I do? What should I do?

Dorothy May was in the middle of her senior year and was one project away from completing the requirements for her diploma at the Tennessee Agricultural and Industrial College when she received the letter by post from the superintendent of the Clarksville Board of Education. She almost had her degree. But she was being offered a position, in her hometown, to do what she had been training to do the past four years.

If I don't take it, someone else surely will. And how many years before there is another position at the Clarksville Colored School—decades, maybe?

As Dorothy May waited for the sound of the dinner bell, she looked out across the courtyard. Students were walking back to the dormitories from classes. Couples were standing under the large oak trees, heads close, talking and laughing.

If I leave school to take the teaching job in Clarksville, I will miss all of this: the quiet bustle of the campus; the peaceful view from my window. But life goes on and things change.

The dinner bell rang.

Dorothy May gathered at table number nine with Hazel, Arthurine, Sarah, Maddie, and Mary Jean. They had managed, even finagled, over the years to be assigned to the same table. Their friendship was rooted around their daily interactions over dinner. Dorothy May planned to share the contents of the letter with them. If they agreed she should leave school and take the job, then she would do it.

When Mrs. Cullen, the housemother, finished saying grace and sat down at the head table, the friends passed around the serving dishes.

"You know, Mrs. Cullen rushes through grace like she can't wait to start eating," Maddie said as she passed along the meat platter.

"That may be, but she doesn't patrol the parlor like a drill sergeant during evening visiting hours," Arthurine said.

"Why, last Sunday, she let Charlotte and her young man sit there on the sofa and hold hands," Sarah whispered. "I saw it with my own eyes."

"No, you don't say," Dorothy May said.

"I think she likes to see young people courting," Hazel said.

"Well, there's nothing wrong with that. Where are you supposed to find a husband if you can't find him in school?" Maddie asked. "I hope to be engaged by the time we get our diplomas."

Mary Jean asked, "Are you getting that serious with Roy? Really?"

"Shhh!" Maddie said. "Don't say a word to anyone!"

"Well, Hazel, what about you and your young man?" Sarah asked.

"Edgar? He's so shy, he won't even come visit me in the parlor," Hazel said.

"Shy? Why I see the way he looks at you when you walk into Oratory class," Arthurine said. "Nothing shy about the look in his eyes!"

Mary Jean looked at Dorothy May. "Hasn't anyone caught your eye since we've been up here?" she asked her.

"Mary Jean's right, Dorothy May," Hazel said. "I don't think you've done any courting since we've been here."

"Now, you all have asked me that before and my answer is the same: I don't have time for that," Dorothy May said. "I came up here to study. I was blessed to be here, and I don't want to ever let it be said that I wasn't grateful for the opportunity or didn't take full advantage of the education here."

"Well, we're all grateful to be here," Maddie said. "But surely someone's caught your eye?"

Dorothy May gave Maddie a stern look.

"I see that look Dorothy May gave Maddie. We'd best change the subject," Sarah said.

"Dorothy May, you've looked distracted since we sat down at the table—and I know it's not about courting! What's on your mind?" Hazel asked.

"Well, there is something I wanted to share with you all. I received this letter in today's post," Dorothy May said, pulling the letter out of her skirt pocket. She read the contents of the letter in a low voice and then waited for the women to respond.

"Oh, Dorothy May," Hazel said, clearly distressed. "You can't leave us!"

"Oh yes she can," Maddie said. "That is a wonderful opportunity. It means that the folks in Clarksville have been keeping up with your progress here at Tennessee A&I. They think you're ready for your own classroom. You can't say no, Dorothy May!"

Dorothy May looked at her other friends and asked, "Arthurine? Sarah? Mary Jean? Do you agree?"

The three of them nodded their heads.

"Maddie's right," Mary Jean said. "This is an opportunity that may never come again. How many teachers have they had at that colored schoolhouse—I'm guessing two? Maybe three?"

"But I'm so close to getting my degree!" Dorothy May said.

"And you will get that degree, I know you will," Sarah said. "But now you have a school that needs you, in your hometown, no less. You have to say yes!"

"All of you are right," Dorothy May said. "I know you are. It's just that I love it here. And I love you all . . ." Dorothy put a handkerchief up to her eyes to blot away the tears. Then she said, "First thing tomorrow morning, I'll make an appointment to see Dean Conrad to tell him I won't be finishing out the school year."

That evening, Dorothy May sat at her desk and wrote a letter of reply to the superintendent of the Clarksville Board of Education. It began:

"Dear Superintendent: I am happy to accept your offer to serve as the teacher at the Clarksville Colored School . . ."

As the teacher in the colored schoolhouse, it had not taken Dorothy May long to learn how to blend the rhythm of her students' lives into the demands of the school year. Most of her students were from farm families, and the main crop in the farms surrounding Clarksville, Tennessee, was tobacco. During the fall, during "cutting time," her classroom would be practically empty. Even though their families did not own the land, every child, if they could walk and breathe, was expected to work the field, cutting the stalks of tobacco so that they could wilt in the sun.

During this time—in addition to their basic lessons—Dorothy May created little projects for those children who were still in class. That fall, she taught her students to make delicate, colorful flowers from crepe paper. They made roses, poppies, daisies, and others of no particular variety. They were all lovely. So much so that Reverend Wilkins, pastor of Mt. Zion Baptist Church, agreed that Dorothy May and her students could sell them, with the proceeds benefitting the school, at the church's annual harvest picnic.

On Sunday, Dorothy May arrived at the picnic grounds by the Cumberland River and was immediately escorted by a deacon to the head table for the main meal. Protocol dictated seating the teacher next to the preacher or, if the preacher was married, next to the preacher's wife. She had begun to dread it anytime she was led to the seat of honor. She was now thirty-two years old, and she was beginning to feel like the honored spinster, especially if other dignitaries—fraternal officers, elected officials, and the like—were accompanied by their wives and seated next to her in the seats of honor.

"Hello, Reverend Wilkins, Mrs. Wilkins," Dorothy May said, nodding at each before she took her seat. She caught herself in that decades-old habit of turning her face to the right as she greeted the couple.

That darn scar!

She straightened her face and looked at the couple directly.

"Good afternoon, Miss Jackson. We are honored that you and your students could join us this afternoon," Reverend Wilkins replied.

Dorothy May was served a heaping plate of grilled rabbit, corn on the cob, bean salad, and cornbread. And then, after eating until she was more than full, she excused herself to gather her students and set up the table for the sale of the flowers.

Dorothy May was glad she could busy herself with her students and the flowers that afternoon. Before long, people were crowded around the table, maneuvering to the front to be able to see the flowers.

"Miss Jackson, this is such a lovely rose, I'm sure you must have made it," said one of the church members.

"No, indeed, the students made all of these flowers themselves," Dorothy May said.

"How much is it?" someone asked.

"I want several of these to set in a vase on my dining room table," said another.

In no time, all but a few tiny flowers had been sold. A man who Dorothy had not seen before came up to the table and said, "I'll buy the rest of these flowers."

"Why, thank you sir, that's very generous of you," Dorothy May said. She looked up and saw a man whose skin was dark brown, almost black. He spoke with a deep, smooth voice with inflections that told her he wasn't from around there.

"Thank you for supporting the children and the school. Are you visiting Clarksville? I don't think I recognize your face."

"Yes, I'm visiting. But you may know my name. I've been corresponding with your mother for a while now. My name is Douglas Ford from New Orleans, Louisiana. And you are Dorothy May Jackson."

Yes, Dorothy May had heard his name. She also knew that her mother was playing matchmaker. Her mother had told her that Douglas Ford would be coming to visit her. "It's time you got married, Dorothy May. Patsy and Addie are married. Have children. You can't teach your whole life away," her mother had said.

"Of course, my mother has mentioned your name. But I had no idea you were coming up to Clarksville today!" Dorothy May said.

"Your mother thought it might be better if you didn't know I was coming ahead of time. Sorry for the surprise," Douglas said.

Mama, you are one devious woman!

"No, I don't mind, really! It's just that I'm here with my students."

"And I've just bought the last of your flowers. So it looks like your duties are finished!"

He extended the crook of his arm toward Dorothy May. "Perhaps we can find a shady spot where we can sit and talk for a bit," Douglas said, pointing to a big oak tree.

Dorothy May put her arm in his. She glanced over her shoulder and saw Mrs. Wilkins's eyes on her.

Go ahead and whisper about me to the Ladies Guild at church, go ahead now. For goodness' sake, I'm good and grown, not some silly-headed young girl!

"I see some of the young folks with baskets, do you see them over there?" she asked, pointing in the opposite direction. "They'll be going what we call 'nutting' along the river. Why don't we join them? We can talk while we gather up nuts. There should be lots of hickory and walnuts on the ground this time of year."

"Sure, if that's what you'd like to do," Douglas said.

It had been quite some time since Dorothy May had gone nutting. It pained her to think about it, but at a certain point, the young men stopped coming to call.

Did Mrs. Shelby scare them away with her talk of me being her "esteemed teacher?" Was it this scar on my face? Or the whispers about my lineage?

Dorothy May Jackson pushed those thoughts out of her head as she and Douglas Ford talked and walked along the river, gathering nuts that had fallen to the ground.

Look at me—here at the picnic, going nutting again with the young people. If only Maddie and Hazel and Mary Jean—all my friends from college—if only they could see me now. Courting at my age!

Their conversation went back and forth, covering various seasons in their lives.

"I have one more project before I get my diploma from Tennessee A&I," Dorothy May explained.

"I was a chauffeur and cook for a widow in New Orleans," said Douglas Ford. "Her husband was a rich merchant in the city. He owned several businesses. She paid me well, and I was able to save enough to start a business."

"I teach in the same one-room schoolhouse I attended when I was a young student."

"I was educated by the Sisters of the Blessed Sacrament. They started a school for the colored children in New Orleans."

"I have a sewing machine—a treadle machine they call it—and I sew most of my own clothes."

"I'm starting a wood-hauling business in Detroit."

"Detroit? Why there?"

"There are a lot of automobile factories there. I've got it all planned out: I take the wooden crates that their parts are shipped in, break them down. I have a big old what they call a donkey saw in the lot next to the house—did I tell you I'm building a house?"

Dorothy May shook her head.

"Well, I am. Yes, and at any rate, I use the saw to cut the pieces into firewood and sell the wood in the city and the areas around Detroit. Folks can use it in the wood-burning stoves; they'll always need plenty of wood for cooking and heating their houses. I think it can be a successful business."

"Detroit—that's a long way from here."

"It's not such a long drive from Clarksville. Nice train ride, too."

They walked a bit more and stopped under a large shade tree. The rest of the group had moved on and were still gathering nuts.

"Dorothy May, what I'm telling you is that I'm ready to settle down. I told you I'm building a house. Well, I want a real home and a family. You and I, we're cousins—third or fourth cousins, your mother told me. We have a ready-made history. Our families know each other. I would be honored if you would consider joining me in Detroit as my wife and start a new life with me."

"Douglas Ford—this has been a mighty . . ." Dorothy May was at a loss for words.

Good Lord, what do I say? To go from feeling like the "honored spinster" to receiving a wedding proposal, all in one day! Who would have thought.

Douglas smiled. "I know this is quick and all."

"I just met you today," she said. "My mother knows you, that's for certain, but surely you can't expect an answer today. You understand that I can't answer right now."

"I didn't expect I would get an answer today. I'm going to Detroit to work on the house and get things situated with the business. I'll be returning in a few weeks. May I see you again?"

"Yes, I would like to talk again when you come back. I have a room at Mrs. Shelby's boardinghouse in Colored Town. Anyone you meet on the street can direct you. You may call for me there."

"Miss Dorothy May," he said, making a slight bow, "it has been my pleasure to spend time with you this afternoon."

"Thank you, Mr. Ford. My pleasure, likewise."

He walked her back to the head table at the picnic grounds.

"Mama! You could have told me that you'd invited Douglas Ford to the picnic," Dorothy May said to Addie, rushing over to where her mother stood over the kitchen sink cutting up a chicken.

"Why, what difference would it have made as long as you got to meet him?" her mother answered, putting down her knife and rinsing her hands in the dishpan. "So, tell me, what did you think?"

"He's a very nice man. A businessman," Dorothy May said. "He got straight to the point: He wants to settle down in Detroit. He wants to marry me."

"And what did you say?" her mother asked.

"I told him I couldn't answer right then. He said he's going to Detroit but that he'd return to Clarksville and we could talk again. Mama . . ."

"Dorothy May, I've told you time and time again, you should get on with your life. Get married, start a family. Douglas is a very nice, hardworking man. You could make a good life together. You won't get many offers like that. Don't let this one pass you by."

"Oh, Mama . . . you might as well call me an old maid!"

"Don't be silly, child. But you've given that school and those children enough good years of your life. They'll find someone else to take your place, you can be sure of that. That college of yours is full of good teachers. They'll find another one, just like they found you." Then she added, "You deserve more than living your life tucked away in Mrs. Shelby's boardinghouse."

"But, Mama—" Dorothy May interrupted.

"Shhh—let me finish. You have choices I never had." Addie paused a moment, looking down at the kitchen floor. "Come over here, let's sit down and talk." She took Dorothy May by the arm and led her into the living room. They sat down on the sofa.

"I never had much time for courting," Addie began, her gaze focused just past Dorothy May. "Too busy working, first the fields and then laundry. It was hard work—real hard work. Then when your daddy, Willie Jackson, came along . . . I didn't know much about him. Not much to know, really. Just that he was a quiet man, nice enough. He asked, and I just married him."

Dorothy May fidgeted as she listened to her mother.

Addie said, "Then, when I was working in old Mrs. Beatty's boardinghouse, Tom Mitchell had a room there and he took a fancy to me."

Dorothy May was stunned. The mention of that man's name was enough to make her sit stock still.

Mama's never, ever talked to me like that about the judge.

"There's no getting around our Southern ways. For colored women especially, there's no getting around it. I had no choice with the judge. It was not my decision to make. Not every colored woman has to face what I did, but the burden was placed on me and you girls were born. Willie had no choice either. He bore up the best he could. Wasn't until the judge died that Willie was free to do what he wanted. I figure that's why he took that bit of inheritance and up and moved to Memphis."

Dorothy May watched as her mother took a deep breath.

All these years, Mama, why are you telling me this after all these years?

"I held no hard feelings," Addie continued. "He worked awhile cleaning offices before he died." Then Addie put her hands on Dorothy May's shoulders and looked her straight in the eyes. "Listen to me, Dorothy May. He favored you."

"Who, Mama?"

"The judge, Tom Mitchell, he favored you. He told me—the last time I talked to him, just before your father started working as his porter—he said he wanted you to be the best that a colored woman can be. He told me that. And you've done that. You would have made him proud. You've made me proud. But now, you have a chance to move on. A good man has asked you to marry him. Get on with your life. Make more of your life than you can down here."

Dorothy May stood up.

The best a colored woman can be, that's what he wanted for me . . . that's why he provided for me.

Dorothy sighed deeply. They were both silent.

Then Dorothy May said, looking down at her mother, "Mama, if I do this . . . if I marry Douglas Ford and move with him to Detroit, my heart will always be in Clarksville."

"You'll feel that way for a while, Dorothy May, but give it time," Addie said. "That will change, too."

1929

Good Hair

May Ford wailed as she reached back, arms flailing, trying to grab the posts of the massive oak bed. Her arms could not reach them.

"Here, Mrs. Ford," Mrs. Barker said as she stood over her and leaned in close. "Here, grab my hands . . . hold on tight. Now push. Push!"

May heard the bedroom door open.

"Look!" screamed Patsy. "Look at the blood! There's blood on Mama's sheets!"

"Mama!" Laura said.

May Ford was covered by her long flannel gown, but the blood was showing from the sheets underneath her. May bent her head forward and looked over at her two girls standing in the doorway. "Good Lord," she murmured through gritted teeth. "Girls . . ." she said, her voice strained from the push. "Girls, please . . ."

Mrs. Barker cut her off. "Patsy, take your sister and you two get back in the living room. Go on now!"

"Daddy said the baby's going to be born today. He said since it wasn't a Christmas baby, he said it's going to be born the day after Christmas. That's what Daddy said," Patsy said.

"Baby coming," Laura said.

May closed her eyes as she squeezed Mrs. Barker's hands and pushed.

"Girls, go on now, I'll tell you when the baby's here," Mrs. Barker said.

"How does the baby come out of Mama's belly?" Patsy asked.

"Mrs. Barker . . ." May said, panting. "The girls . . ."

"I'll take care of it. You just keep pushing." Then in a stern voice she said, "Girls, you have to go now!"

"But we want to see the baby come," Patsy said.

"Dear Jesus," May said as the pain's grip subsided.

"Girls!" It was Douglas Ford. "Girls, have mercy, how long have you been in here?" he asked as he raced into the room.

"Douglas," May said, barely panting as she raised her head up off the stack of pillows. Douglas stared at May, at the bloody sheets, then at the girls standing in the doorway.

"It's all right, Douglas," May said, letting out a deep breath. Douglas firmly grasped Patsy's shoulder and then scooped Laura up in his other arm. "We want to see the baby," Patsy said looking up at her father.

"You girls come right back into the living room with your brother. Don't you go wandering off like that. You have plenty to do, playing with all your Christmas toys," he said to them.

"But the baby—" Patsy started.

"Never you mind about that baby," he said to Patsy outside the bedroom. "We'll all see the baby soon enough, I'm sure of it."

Mrs. Barker rushed over behind him and shut the door. "All right, now," she said, looking over at May and leaning against the door. "You rest a bit now," she said. "I'm going to put some fresh sheets underneath you."

May Ford returned the gaze as Mrs. Barker looked her straight in the eye. "Mrs. Ford, you know what you have to do. This is your fourth baby. You know you've got to push to get it out. You act like you don't want to see this child born."

"I don't," May answered.

"Oh, don't be silly."

"I don't want this baby," May said flatly. "After Laura was born, I told Douglas three's enough. I told him I didn't want any more babies," she said, squirming as she talked.

"Oh, Mrs. Ford," Mrs. Barker said. "You're just saying this now. Just wait until you hold that sweet baby in your arms."

May pressed her head back against the pillows and closed her eyes.

Now Laura, that baby was a welcome child.

May smiled at the thought.

"There you go, Mrs. Ford. You just rest . . ." Mrs. Barker said.

Yes, we almost named that baby Welcome. Welcome, what a name that would have been.

May chuckled softly.

Douglas, he insisted that our firstborn, the boy, be a junior. And that was fine with me. Then Patsy, I wanted her named after my sister. And Laura we ended up naming after my mother's mother.

"We almost named that baby Welcome," May said out loud, eyes still shut tight.

"What's that, Mrs. Ford?" Mrs. Barker asked.

May didn't respond. She kept to her thoughts.

We were just so glad to have her because 1927 was such a good year for us. It was such a good year for the business . . . I can hear the phone ringing now. Calls—calls for the Douglas Ford Wood Company—coming in all day long, every day. We had orders for wood for a whole year. The ledger was full. Why, no sooner had I put the receiver down from one call then the phone would ring again. Folks placing orders. Douglas could barely keep up filling the orders. There were hardly enough of the wooden crates at those automobile factories for him and his men to tear apart and haul back to the wood yard.

"Poor Douglas," May murmured, her eyes still closed.

He worked so hard. He worked all alone to cut the wood up with that donkey saw of his. He wouldn't let anyone else touch that saw . . . Said he didn't trust anyone else to work that saw and get the wood cut to just the right size.

"He cut so much wood it would be piled up almost as high as the roof of our house." May opened her eyes and made eye contact with Mrs. Barker. Then she squirmed and grabbed herself tight beneath her belly. She held her breath.

"Mrs. Ford, don't try to talk," Mrs. Barker said. "Just lie still."

May let out her breath and kept talking.

"Douglas and his drivers, they made deliveries all across the city, driving out to Grosse Pointe, out Gratiot to 10 Mile Road—" May screamed, flailing as she was gripped by another deep, sharp pain.

"Steady, Mrs. Ford, steady now. Grab hold to me and push. You've got to push," Mrs. Barker coached her.

"I don't want to! I don't want this baby!" May answered firmly. Then she panted. She moaned.

"I know you don't mean it, Mrs. Ford. Women say a lot of things when they're birthing a child. I know you don't mean it," Mrs. Barker said, wiping a wet towel across May's forehead. May looked straight ahead as the pain lessened.

That woman doesn't understand how hard it was on me after Laura was born. A new baby and two young ones under foot. Patsy was two years old then. Doug Jr. was four. Always a stack of diapers to wash. Little ones to feed. Nursing the newborn. Crying, one of them always crying. And the phone ringing. Answering the telephone. Taking orders. Folks coming by to use the phone.

May Ford swatted Mrs. Barker's arm. "Stop touching me with that towel! Stop it!"

"All right, Mrs. Ford," the woman answered. "I'm just trying to make you more comfortable, that's all."

"Well just stop it, you make me lose my train of thought!" May said. "Where was I? Good Lord, you make it so I can't even think straight."

May felt a fierce muscle cramp squeeze across her lower belly. She moaned and grabbed tight at the sheets beneath her.

Douglas . . . Douglas said . . . he said be neighborly. We've been blessed, he said, no one else around here has a telephone. Be neighborly. But it was on me to make them understand that we're running a business here. They just can't come barging in to use the phone any old time of day and night. Unless it's a fire or they need to call a doctor . . .

"Oh Lord, oh Lord . . . oh my LORD!" May cried out loud. Then she raised her head and looked around her.

She asked Mrs. Barker, "Who's that howling?"

"Steady now, Mrs. Ford," the midwife answered. "The pain's a bit rough now . . ."

Oh my God, that's me. That's me making that racket.

She sank her head back into the pillows.

Good God, why is this happening to me? I told Douglas, no more. No more babies after Laura . . . But Maddie told me how it would be. She told me in her letters—she said once the babies start, there's no stopping them. She told me that. Once she married Roy she was with child in no time, and she said it broke her heart that she had to stop teaching. She's got five now. I can't keep count. Maybe it's six. But they keep coming, Maddie said.

May reached out and grabbed Mrs. Barker's hand. "Maddie?"

"Who?" the midwife asked.

"Oh." May peered more closely at the woman's face. It was Mrs. Barker. "Oh, nothing," May said.

Where's Maddie? I miss my friends. I miss Maddie and Hazel. My friends from Tennessee A&I. Maddie and Hazel—my dear friends. We write letters back and forth now. But it's not the same. I've got no

*one to really talk to up here. Oh the neighborhood women are nice
and polite. The women on each side of us . . . Eva Yablonski, with
that heavy Polish accent: Hello, Meesees Ford. Nice weather, don't
you tink? And then Cleota Chambers—her house is right there next to
the wood yard. Sadie Carson just across the street. They're both from the
South like most of the colored folks around here. Come to find out,
Sadie's from Montgomery County, just up the river from Clarksville.
Lord, Lord . . .*

May felt a hand grip the space down below her belly.

"Don't touch me there!" she yelled at Mrs. Barker.

"The baby's head . . . I can almost touch it!" the woman said.

"No, don't, please don't. Just leave me alone!" May pleaded.
"Please leave me alone!"

She sank back into her thoughts.

*Nice enough women, all of them. But they don't understand. Not
like Maddie and Hazel . . . No one I can really talk to . . .*

May wailed as another deep pain gripped her. Before she knew
it, she was pushing down and pushing hard.

"There you go, keep pushing! This baby isn't going to wait much
longer," Mrs. Barker said.

The midwife's face was close to May's face. May could feel her
breath, could feel the spit coming from her mouth every time the
woman said push. The woman's hand, she could feel her big hand
as she talked.

"The baby's head is down so low now, you've got to help it.
Come on now . . ." Mrs. Barker said.

"God, no!" May cried. "Why is this happening?" May couldn't
help but push.

*Why is this happening? That's what I said—early spring—when
I knew I had another baby coming. They keep coming. That's what
Maddie said to me. The babies keep coming and there's nothing you
can do about it. Except—and Maddie said don't tell a soul—her
daddy with his funeral business and all, he showed Maddie the body*

of a woman who tried to stop the baby from coming. Before she mar-
ried Roy, he showed her when he brought the body in. Don't do it, her
daddy told her. You see what happens? You take what comes, he told
her. So that's all we can do, Maddie said to me. Just take what comes.

"There you go," Mrs. Barker said. "Now you're helping things along here."

"No, not now," May wailed.

Not now! I told Douglas. This can't be happening now. He turned
on the radio to get more news about the crash. The stock market crash,
he said it was. Not with the baby almost here, I said. I said, I knew
it was wrong to have this baby! Douglas turned to me. He had a look
of shock on his face. He grabbed me by the shoulders. Don't you ever
think anything like that again! We'll be fine, he told me. We'll make
it, just like we always have. That child will have everything it needs.
Just like the rest of our children . . .

"You're doing fine," the midwife said.

"That's what my husband said," May said, panting.

"What's that, now?" Mrs. Barker asked.

Breathless, May said, "Black Tuesday. The day of the crash. We'll do fine, he said to me. People will still need wood. They still have to keep warm and cook dinner on a hot stove. We'll do fine, he said." She moaned.

"And here you are and look at you—you almost birthed a Christmas baby!" Mrs. Barker said.

"Nothing will be the same," May said dryly. Then she tensed up, grabbing herself under her belly.

"I'll say," the midwife said. "You'll have four young ones under foot. You'll be one busy mama. Now come on, Mrs. Ford. Let's bring this baby home!"

May closed her eyes and felt the muscles in her abdomen and inner thighs squeeze tight and push down on their own.

"I've got hold of the head!" Mrs. Barker said.

May almost sat straight up in the bed. She leaned forward,

knees spread wide apart, and looked down below her belly. She watched as Mrs. Barker cradled the baby's head in her open hands.

"Come on, the baby's almost here. One more push and we're done. There you go! Yes, I do believe you're done. Lord have mercy, you did it. You have a beautiful baby girl!"

Mrs. Barker reached over and took hold of a small knife and cut the umbilical cord. Then she turned the baby over and gently whacked the child's bottom. The baby wailed.

"There you go, precious one," the midwife said. She leaned over to place the baby at May's breast.

"Hold your little girl while I get the afterbirth. Just push a little bit more for me."

"I don't want to hold the baby," May Ford said, looking at Mrs. Barker but not at the baby.

Still holding the child, Mrs. Barker turned toward the bedroom door, but Douglas Ford had already opened the door and was walking in.

"I heard a baby cry!" he said, smiling as he entered the room. Before he closed the door, he called over his shoulder, "Children, you get back in the living room. You can see the new baby soon enough!"

"Yes, Mr. Ford," Mrs. Barker said, "you have a lovely baby daughter."

"May," he said, taking her hands in his as he knelt by the side of the bed. He leaned forward and kissed her on the forehead. Then he got up and stood by Mrs. Barker. She had wrapped the little one in a small blanket.

"Mr. Ford, I'll need you to hold your daughter while I tend to the afterbirth," she said while handing him the child. "It'll just be a moment."

Mrs. Barker pressed down on May's abdomen.

"Stop, that's enough!" May cried as she raised her hips, grabbing at the sheets beneath her.

"There, that's all it took. That's it. We're done here. You birthed your baby!"

"I don't want the baby," May said as she curled her knees up to her stomach and turned to face the wall, away from Douglas and Mrs. Barker.

"May, you don't mean that! Here, turn around and hold the baby," Douglas said, leaning forward with the baby still in his arms. "Put her to your breast. We have another daughter," he said softly.

"No, Douglas, no," May moaned. "Mrs. Barker, tell him."

"Shhh, shhh, shhh, Mrs. Ford," Mrs. Barker said. She looked at Douglas Ford and lowered her voice. "I've seen this happen before. She'll snap out of it. Birthing's a hard business. Sometimes this happens. It'll pass. Right now, I'm going to get the child cleaned up. I've got a basin over here." She took the baby from Douglas Ford's arms. "But I need you to go boil some water. We'll have to feed the baby some sugar water right now. Then . . . well then if Mrs. Ford doesn't snap out of it presently, I'll have to find you a wet nurse."

May Ford heard Doug Jr.'s voice on the other side of the bedroom door as she lay in bed. "Why is Mrs. Brown holding the baby? Why doesn't Mama hold the baby?" the boy asked.

"Let me see the baby," Laura said.

"What's the baby's name? Why doesn't that baby have a name yet?" Patsy asked.

"Now you children go on now. Let Mrs. Brown feed the baby," Douglas said.

"I want to see the baby, too," Patsy said.

"Go on now," their father said. "Mrs. Barker," he started.

"Yes, Mr. Ford," Mrs. Barker said.

Then his voice turned to a whisper.

May Ford heard more whispers outside her bedroom door. Her husband and Mrs. Barker always stood at the door and whispered to each other before they came into the bedroom. May couldn't quite make out what they were saying this time, but she was sure it had to do with that baby. Always that baby.

I don't want that baby. I told them I don't want the girl. I have three beautiful children—one boy and two girls—and I don't want another. I don't need another. Mrs. Barker comes in here, telling me she has to start my milk flowing, telling me she has to get that thick yellow liquid out—the first milk, she called it—so the real milk will come through. But I don't need the real milk. I'm not feeding any baby.

"Get your hands off of me," May cried out.

"Now, Mrs. Ford, you know I have to do this. It's for your own good. For the baby. I've got to get the first milk flowing," Mrs. Barker said as she took firm hold of one breast and squeezed firmly as she pulled down on it. The thick liquid squirted out and onto a towel the midwife had placed under May's breasts.

"Leave me alone," May wailed.

"May, do this for the child," Douglas pleaded in a low voice.

"No, no," May said, pushing Mrs. Barker away.

May felt her husband's hands on her arms as he reached across Mrs. Barker and pinned them down at her side.

"Just a little longer, May," Douglas Ford said softly. "Go ahead, Mrs. Barker."

The midwife placed her hands on the other breast. "Your husband's right, just a little longer, that's all it'll take."

How long will this go on? The pain, the bother. Always something to do with the baby. Just take the baby. Take it somewhere and leave me alone.

May started to doze off. But she heard her husband talking to Mrs. Barker.

"It's been three days now. Three days that child has been without her mother," Douglas said.

"I've seen this happen before. She'll snap out of it. Till then, Mrs. Brown's doing a good job of nursing the baby."

"She's not the mother."

"Babies have sucked at the breast of a wet nurse since the beginning of time. Your little girl will be fine."

"It's not just the child I'm thinking about. I don't want any gossip getting around the neighborhood."

"Mrs. Brown won't say a word about nursing the child. As far as anyone around here knows, she's just coming over here to help out with the young ones and the cooking and cleaning."

"You're sure about that?"

"I talked to her from the start. She knows better; she won't say a word. And in the meantime, I'll think of something. Something to snap your wife out of it. It happens, Mr. Ford. Birthing is hard on a woman. Strange thoughts can go through their head. Sometimes, this kind of thing just happens."

The talk stopped. May fell asleep.

When May woke up, she didn't know if it was the same day or if she had slept through the night. Mrs. Barker was sitting next to her, staring down at her. The children were quiet. She didn't hear sounds of the baby crying.

Something's wrong. It's too quiet. Something's not right.

"You're awake now," Mrs. Barker said, smiling down at May Ford.

May shifted her body more to her left, directly facing Mrs. Barker. She noticed that the woman had a hairbrush in her hand.

"What are you doing? Is something wrong? Why are you holding that brush? That's my brush . . ." May said, sounding more and more anxious with each question. She reached toward the brush.

"Shhh. Shhh. Calm down now. Nothing's wrong. Here, have a drink of water." Mrs. Barker reached over to the nightstand and grabbed a glass of water. She helped May sit up and put the glass to her lips.

"This is a beautiful brush. Inlaid mother of pearl on the head. My my . . . I've never seen anything like it," the woman said.

"My husband gave it to me. A gift after Doug Jr. was born," May said.

"It's beautiful. Just like your hair," Mrs. Barker said. "Here, scoot to the side a bit and let me sit down next to you. I want to brush your hair for you. You have such lovely hair. All the neighbor women admire it, Mrs. Ford, you know that don't you?" The midwife began working the brush down May's wavy, black hair, from the top of her head to where it stopped halfway down her back.

"I could sit on my hair when I married Douglas, it was that long," May said as she tilted her head back. "Can you imagine that? I could sit on it. Of course, I always twisted it up into a bun of some kind when I went out in public. Still do. Down South or up North, that's just the proper thing to do."

May was silent as Mrs. Barker continued her long strokes with the brush. It had been a long time since anyone else had brushed her hair.

Goodness, I'm so used to taking care of others—Douglas, the children, my students down in Clarksville. It's nice to have someone tending to me. Brushing my hair.

"Your daughters have a nice grade of hair," Mrs. Barker said.

May's back stiffened. "Ornery colored hair, that's what those girls have. Not wiry like their father's, no. But ornery just the same."

"Oh Mrs. Ford . . ."

"Now, we're pleased with the children's color—not as dark as Douglas but not as bright as me. A nice brown color, like you, Mrs. Barker."

"Why yes, nice . . . brown," Mrs. Barker said.

"But that ornery colored hair . . ." May said, shaking her head. "You know, after Douglas and I were first married and I was carrying our first child, I used to daydream that the baby was already born and that it was a little girl. I could see myself sitting behind her, just like you're behind me now, brushing her long black hair."

"You can still do that, Mrs. Ford," Mrs. Barker said, still brushing May's hair.

"Don't you know? I can barely get a comb through their thick, ornery hair. I just give them two braids, one on each side. That's all I can do. Maybe when they're older—"

"That's not what I meant," Mrs. Barker interrupted. She stopped brushing.

"What are you talking about?" May asked.

"Your baby girl. That little one has good hair, Mrs. Ford."

It's that baby, again. She's talking about that baby.

"She's your baby. You birthed her. And she was born with a head full of beautiful curly hair. You can sit behind her and brush it, just like you've always dreamed." Mrs. Barker was still talking.

My baby, she says. Yes, I birthed her. She's my baby.

"My baby?" May asked. She paused. "My little girl has beautiful hair?"

I always dreamed of brushing my girls' long beautiful hair. Now Mrs. Barker says my baby girl has good hair. That I can sit and brush her beautiful hair . . .

"Yes, indeed, Mrs. Ford. Yes she does. Do you want to see her?" Mrs. Barker asked. She placed the brush on the nightstand.

"Just take her in your arms. Put her up to your breast. You can touch her hair while she sucks at your breast."

"She has good hair?" May asked.

"Yes she does, Mrs. Ford. I wouldn't lie to you. Let me bring the baby to you," Mrs. Barker said. "Just sit back here against the pillows. I'll bring her to you."

Mrs. Barker fluffed up the pillows. Then she left the room and closed the door.

Whispers. I hear whispers. Who's that woman talking to? What is she saying? Is she talking about the baby?

The whispers stopped.

Mrs. Barker returned with the baby wrapped in a thick, white blanket.

"Here she is," Mrs. Barker said. "Here's your daughter."

It's my baby, she says. She says my daughter has good hair.

"Do you want to hold her?" Mrs. Barker asked, coming closer. "Do you want to see her hair?" She pulled the blanket off the child's head.

Dear God look at that—the baby girl has a head full of beautiful hair! I thought that old midwife was lying to me about the child having good hair. She was telling the truth.

"Won't you hold her, Mrs. Ford?"

Mrs. Barker stood beside the bed, the baby in her arms. The child started whimpering.

May Ford looked over at the baby squirming in Mrs. Barker's arms, with a head full of black curly hair.

"Mrs. Ford . . . Mrs. Ford?"

May shook her head and blinked her eyes, as if waking up from a dream. Then she stared at the child, stared hard.

Oh my Lord, look at that hair! That's the baby girl I birthed.

May Ford hesitated.

I birthed her. She's my child. Head full of hair. Look at her . . . look at that dear child!

May slowly reached out her arms. Mrs. Barker handed the baby girl to her, still holding onto the child as she did so.

"Oh, she's a lively little thing, isn't she," May said as the baby squirmed in her arms. Mrs. Barker let go of the child as May steadied the baby in the crook of her elbow. May pulled the baby to her breast. She hesitated, then she touched the child's hair.

"There you go, little one," she said to the baby, as Mrs. Barker looked on. "There you go," she said as the baby settled down and started to suck. May Ford pulled the child even closer to her and looked down at the baby girl.

Beautiful hair. Yes, indeed. Beautiful hair.

May gently stroked the baby's hair.

I birthed you. You're my child.

9

1946

DAY WORK

May Ford rapped hard against the kitchen window, trying to get Laura's attention as she walked up the driveway. But Laura jumped at the sound, and May watched as her daughter, startled by the noise, lost her footing and fell forward.

"Good God," May murmured, "that child never could walk a straight line . . ."

Laura caught her balance before she hit the ground, but her schoolbooks slipped out of her arms and onto the driveway. Laura looked up at her mother in the window as she kneeled and gathered her books. May Ford was waving an envelope in her hand.

"Hurry up!" she said, even though she knew Laura could barely hear her through the glass.

Laura nodded.

May Ford was standing in the kitchen, still waving a letter in her hand, as Laura entered through the back door.

"Goodness, child, I thought you'd never get home!" May said. "Jean's been home almost a half hour. Where have you been?"

"It's such a nice day that I—" Laura explained before her mother cut her off.

"Never mind, never mind," May said. "Look at this. This letter came for you. I saw that it was from the University of Michigan and opened it. Look at this!" May said, handing Laura the letter with such force that the girl almost dropped her books again.

"OK, let me see . . . let me put my books down," Laura said, grabbing the paper with her free hand while she let her books fall onto a kitchen chair.

Laura quickly glanced at the front and back of the letter and then read out loud, "May 1, 1946, Office of Scholarships and Financial Aid, University of Michigan, Ann Arbor, Michigan, Dear Miss Ford: Congratulations on having received notice of your acceptance to the University of Michigan, class of 1950, two weeks ago. Based upon your superior scholastic standing in your graduating class at Pershing High School, Detroit, Michigan, the University of Michigan is pleased to offer you a four-year scholarship in the College of Literature, Science and the Arts. Please indicate your intent to either accept or decline this scholarship offer by signing your name in the space provided at the bottom of this page and returning the bottom portion of this letter to us by June 1, 1946. We look forward to hearing from you. Yours truly . . ."

Laura waved the letter above her head. "Mother, now can I attend the University of Michigan?" Laura asked. "Mother?"

Laura, her second oldest daughter, had also received a letter of acceptance from Wayne University there in Detroit. And, like her brother, Doug, and older sister, Patsy, she had been offered a merit award from that university covering tuition for the first two years.

"I just want to see if I can get in," Laura gave as her reason as she completed the application to the University of Michigan, sitting at the kitchen table. "It's one of the top schools in the country,

Mama, and I just want to see if I can rank high enough to get in, that's all."

May never dreamed Laura would be accepted into the university.

Good Lord, I never thought anything would come of it, even when she received that letter of admission. Douglas and I saved for their college educations all these years, me walking to the post office, faithfully adding money to their accounts each week. Neighbors would ask as I walked by, What are you doing at the post office, Mrs. Ford? I made sure they understood the way of it. We were saving for their future.

May shook her head and she looked over at Laura as the girl looked down at the letter.

We were saving for the local university. But this scholarship from Michigan . . . this changes everything.

"Laura?" May asked.

Her daughter looked up.

"You really want to leave home, go away to that school?" May asked. "Your father will say that Wayne University is good enough. You know that."

Laura did not answer right away.

"We've held you children close. Didn't let you run up and down the street like most of the other children around here, colored or white," May said to Laura's silence. "We raised you with an eye toward your future. And this is what comes of it. So answer me—do you want to go to this school?"

"Yes, I do, I want to go away to school, to the University of Michigan," Laura answered slowly. "You know not many Negro students are given this opportunity. Yes, I want to do this."

"Then that's where you'll go," her mother said. "I'll talk to your father, alone, when he comes home."

And when he did come home and May told him about the letter, she could hear the irritation in his voice when he asked, "May, what did you tell the child?"

Before she could answer, Douglas left the kitchen and walked toward their bedroom.

"I told her she could go. I told her I'd talk to you," May answered, following close behind him.

Once May was in their bedroom, Douglas shut the door.

"So you told her she could go," Douglas said as he knocked the tobacco out of his pipe and into the ashtray on their dresser.

"What could I say? They're giving her a scholarship. They want her at that university," May said.

"Patsy's set to graduate from Wayne University this spring, I'll grant you that. And Doug graduates next year and then he's off to medical school. Thank God the GI Bill will pay for much of that. But we have Jean coming along and then baby Annie May, Lord willing. Why would we send Laura all the way off to school? It costs money to send a child off to school. We've got a perfectly good school right here."

"They're giving her a scholarship, Douglas," May answered.

"What kind of scholarship, May?"

"The letter said a four-year scholarship. Four years. That's what I know."

May stepped closer to her husband.

"This is what those nuns—"

"Sisters. Sisters of the Blessed Sacrament."

"I don't care what you call them. This is what they wanted when they started that colored school you went to down in New Orleans. They weren't just educating you. They were preparing you to pass it on to your own children, just like we've done."

"Same thing with that judge of yours . . . when he provided for your schooling," Douglas said.

May lowered her head and nodded. "You're right, I don't deny it."

She could hear his loud sigh before Douglas said, "Then tell me this—who's going to take care of her at that University of Michigan? Who's going to watch over her, a Negro girl in a small town like Ann Arbor? Tell me, May. Tell me. We've always been here for them, to help make a way for them, to see them through. We shielded these children from so much, May"—he shook his head—"just by raising them up North. Lord knows it's not perfect up here, but it's nothing like what I knew in New Orleans or what you knew in Clarksville. Now she'll be in a small town, up here, mind you, but a small town just the same, all by herself . . ."

"Doug went across the ocean, fought in Italy. He did fine."

"He was a man, already at the university when he went overseas."

"Still, we raised him the same way. He went over there and he came home a hero," she said.

"That he did."

"We raised her well, Douglas. She can handle herself. And she won't be all alone—she'll be living in the dormitory. And mind you, she won't be the only Negro girl up there, I'm sure of it. She'll be fine."

It was quiet between them.

"And you already told the child she could go," Douglas said, breaking the silence.

"I did."

"I won't ask you to go back on your word," he said.

May watched as he pulled a pouch of tobacco from his pocket and started packing the bowl of his pipe. Then she left the bedroom and went in the kitchen to finish dinner.

It did not take long for word to spread around the rest of the neighborhood.

Laura was with her mother the next day when they talked to their next-door neighbor, Mrs. Cleota Chambers, and then Mrs. Sadie Carson, who lived across the street.

"Well, what do you know," Mrs. Chambers said, grabbing Laura by the shoulders and pulling her into a hug. "You make us proud, Laura. Yes, indeed, you make us proud!"

"Thank you, ma'am," Laura said.

From across the street, Sadie Carson stood up from her chair on the front porch. "I do declare, I hear that little girl's going away to school? Well May, you and Douglas have done a fine job of raising those children. No doubt about it."

"Oh, folks around here are pleased to hear the news about Laura, that's for sure," May shared as the family gathered in the kitchen for dinner later in the week. She looked over at Jean who was taking plates from the cabinet. "Jean, just get out five plates. Doug and Patsy aren't home yet. Looks like they'll be eating on campus today. Laura, put out the silverware. Annie May, napkins, please."

She continued as the family took their seats. "Neighbors were stopping me on the way home, on my way back from Joseph Campau Street when I went to the butcher shop earlier today, asking me if it was true. Congratulating Laura," she said, nodding at Laura. "I don't know if all of them were quite sincere," she added as she started passing around the plate of mashed potatoes and then the bowl of pickled okra.

"How could you tell, Mama?" Jean asked.

"Tone of voice, mostly," her mother answered.

"Huh? Why weren't they sincere?" Laura asked after taking some okra.

"I can answer that easy enough," Douglas Ford said as he took the tongs from the platter and placed a slice of pot roast on each plate. "I can count on one hand the others who are going to college from this neighborhood—Negro or white—much less the whole family of children, and that's a fact," he said. "Probably, some folks can't handle that." Then he asked, "May, is there any gravy for the meat and potatoes?"

"Oh goodness, yes," she said. "Annie?" May looked at Annie and pointed over to the stove.

Annie went to the stove and brought the gravy boat to the table.

"But that's all right," May said as she passed the gravy to her husband. "They've watched me march up to that post office week after week, putting money into each one of their accounts. It was no secret why we put that money away. I told anyone who asked what I was doing and why."

"Um-hum, well it's no secret that I'm ready to eat," Douglas said. "Let's bless the food."

"Mary Andrews, Wilma Harris, Janet Curry, Harriet Farmer . . ."

May Ford had rattled off the list of names to Dr. Hammonds as she sat on his examination table. Those were the names of some of Patsy's friends who had succumbed to tuberculosis just in the year since the war ended. Those names came to mind when, a couple weeks after they had dropped off Laura at the University of Michigan, May had been unable to shake a cough. She felt fine, but she knew a cough could be a sign, a deadly sign, and after a few days of it, she knew she should get to a doctor. Dr. Hammonds was still the only Negro doctor in the area—he had been their family doctor since Doug and Patsy were young—so May rang up his office and told the receptionist about her cough. She was able to see him that day.

Dr. Hammonds lifted the stethoscope from her chest. "You're fine, Mrs. Ford. Your lungs sound clear as a bell. I don't even need to send you for X-rays. You don't have tuberculosis."

"Thank you, doctor! Thank goodness," May said as a smile spread across her face.

"Your throat is a little dry. Probably something in the air causing an irritation of some sort. Just take a teaspoonful of honey or put some in a cup of tea. Something to lubricate your throat."

May nodded.

"But I know what you mean, especially with so many of our

young people dying from the disease. Sometimes I fear that TB might very well decimate an entire generation of the Negro population in the city of Detroit."

Patsy went to see Dr. Hammonds shortly after that. She was a post-graduate student at Wayne University and about to start her student teaching—October 1 was her official start day. She had to have a complete physical examination including a chest X-ray. It was required of all teachers and student teachers by the Detroit Public Schools. So when Dr. Hammonds's nurse called and left a message for Patsy that she was to come to his office, pick up her set of X-rays, and take them not to her school but to Herman Kiefer Hospital, May thought, "If the doctor wants Patsy to take her X-rays to Herman Kiefer he must think . . ."

Herman Kiefer was the shortened name. Everyone in Detroit called it that. The full name was Herman Kiefer County Hospital. May knew that it was the place where the Wayne County birth and death records were kept and where folks went when they needed to get copies of those papers. It was where many poor folks went to receive care when they couldn't afford to go anywhere else. It was also the place where anyone from Detroit and the surrounding cities in Wayne County who was diagnosed with a communicable disease, like tuberculosis, was sent to be treated.

May knew all of this. Her spirit sank as those thoughts went through her head.

"Not tuberculosis . . . TB . . . not my baby, too!" she moaned as she put down the phone and slowly lowered herself onto a kitchen chair.

I should have known . . . the way she looked lately . . . face drawn, shoulders starting to stoop. I should have known . . .

"Let me come with you," May said as she turned to Patsy during breakfast that next morning. "Picking up your films is easy enough, Dr. Hammonds's office being just up the road here on

Dequindre, but the county hospital is such a big place. It's easy to get lost around there."

May and Douglas talked about it one last time before breakfast while they were still in their bedroom. If Dr. Hammonds wanted Patsy to take her X-rays to Herman Kiefer Hospital, then he must think there was a good chance she had TB. If she had TB, then it meant Patsy would not be coming home that day. It meant they would put her straight into the hospital or even send her out to Maybury Sanitarium.

May had heard about Maybury from neighbors and from talking to folks at church. She had heard too many times that people were sent to Maybury Sanitarium not to get better but to die. She had heard all that. But this last time talking it over with Douglas, it hit her hard.

If Patsy's sick enough to be sent out there . . . sweet Jesus!

She slumped down on the side of the bed. She tried not to wail. "Oh Douglas!" she said, her voice trembling. "You know what they say about Maybury . . . Oh dear Lord, my baby!"

Douglas put his hand on her shoulder.

"Yes, we both know what they say. But this will all work out. The Lord didn't bring our family this far to let us down now. I have to believe that. And we don't even know if they'll be sending her to Maybury," he said. He lifted May's face up so that she was looking him straight in the eye. "Shall I come with you and Patsy?" he asked.

May shook her head. "Who's going to cover for you? You've already let go of two drivers. No . . . plus if both of us come then she'll know something's wrong for sure. No need to alarm her right away. You're right, we don't even know ourselves how this will all work out. The doctor at Herman Kiefer might look at the X-rays and say she's fine. No use getting her upset for nothing."

On the morning of October 1, after picking up a large envelope containing the X-ray films from Dr. Hammonds's office, May Ford and Patsy, with envelope in hand, stepped off the bus and walked up to the doors of Herman Kiefer County Hospital. They arrived early enough, May assured her daughter, for Patsy to drop off the films and get to her student teaching post on time. After they finally found the correct department and signed in at the receptionist's window, an orderly stepped into the room, called her name, and asked Patsy and May to follow him. He led them to an elevator, which they rode down to the basement. Then they followed him through a corridor to a parking garage. A large black passenger vehicle was waiting for them. The orderly held open the rear door as they took their seats; there were no other riders. When he closed the door and nodded his head, the driver immediately started the engine and drove off.

"Where are they taking us, Mother? And why isn't anyone else riding with us?" Patsy asked, looking at the other empty seats and sounding a bit anxious and confused.

"We'll know soon enough," her mother replied.

"But I'm supposed to start my student teaching this morning," Patsy reminded her. "Who's going to call my supervisor and tell her I'll be late?"

"We'll take care of it. There's plenty of time," her mother said, trying to sound confident.

It was a long drive, lasting almost an hour. Whenever Patsy asked about the time or questioned where they were going, May quickly changed the subject to gossip about someone in the neighborhood or at church. When they finally arrived, they were outside the city of Detroit and in the small town of Northville Township. The van stopped in front of a large sign that read Maybury Sanitarium. They were met at the door by a nurse who took the envelope from Patsy's hand and directed her to go down one hallway to have another X-ray taken and then directed May Ford down another hallway to a waiting area.

"Let me take your purse," May said to Patsy as her daughter turned to leave. "I'll be waiting for you down the hall."

Almost an hour later, May Ford had already been escorted to Dr. Peck's office when Patsy entered wearing a hospital gown.

"Mother, they've taken my suit," Patsy said as she entered the room. "I told them I'm already late for my student teaching and that I have to have my clothes back."

"Shhh, shhh, sit here," May said, motioning to the chair next to her.

"Mother, what is going on here?" Patsy demanded. "No one will answer my questions. And I keep telling them I'm late already."

Before May could answer, a man wearing a white coat entered the room and sat behind the desk in front of them. He introduced himself as Dr. Peck.

"And hello, Miss Ford," Dr. Peck said, greeting Patsy. "I need to speak to your mother as well."

The doctor scanned Patsy's face, looked over at May, then returned his focus to Patsy.

He sees Patsy's brown skin. He sees my bright color. He's thinking, is this a nurse? A social worker? I know what he's going to say next.

"Is this your . . . moth—?"

"Yes, I'm Mrs. Ford. I'm her mother," May answered, cutting him off before he finished the question.

"Good," he said. He cleared his throat as he put Patsy's chart and films on his desk.

"Miss Ford," he asked, looking directly at Patsy, "how long have you felt sick?"

"Am I sick?"

"Why, yes you are." He picked up the films. "I've examined your X-rays. Both sets. You have rather deep cavities on both lungs. This indicates that you have been sick for quite some time. When did you have your last chest X-rays taken, aside from the ones you've brought with you here?"

Patsy explained to the doctor that she had one taken in February or March of that year. The university required them of all of the students because so many were falling ill.

"You're at the university?"

"Why, yes," Patsy responded. May could hear the defensive tone in her voice. "And you've interrupted the first day of my student teaching schedule."

Dr. Peck said, "Miss Ford, you're going to be staying here for a while."

"Can my mother stay with me?" Patsy asked.

"No," he replied. "No, you'll be staying too long for that."

"But I've got to contact my student teaching supervisor."

Dr. Peck looked concerned. "We'll take care of that. Have you had contact with any children yet?"

"No," Patsy answered. "Not at the school. But until a week or so ago, I worked at the recreation center."

He looked at May Ford. "We'll want to take X-rays of your entire family, and we'll arrange for each child your daughter has had contact with at the recreation center to have an X-ray as well."

May nodded.

Dr. Peck pressed the buzzer on his desk. A nurse entered immediately. "Please take Miss Ford to room 122, bed number two."

Patsy hugged her mother tightly. "What's happening to me, Mother?" she pleaded as she burst into tears.

"Everything will be fine, baby," May whispered as they embraced. "You'll see."

The nurse took Patsy by the elbow, gently pulling her away from her mother, and led her out of the room. May listened to Dr. Peck as he talked, but she kept her eyes on Patsy as she made her way down the hall, escorted by the nurse.

"Your daughter will receive standard treatment: total bed rest. She will lie flat on her back. She cannot sit up for a full year. Of course she can read, she can eat. She will wash herself and use the bedpan. But all of this will be done while lying on her back. Mrs. Ford?"

May briefly turned toward Dr. Peck, nodded, and then turned her gaze back to Patsy.

"Mrs. Ford, anything your daughter has handled at home will have to be either boiled or destroyed." He paused.

Patsy was walking slower now. May could tell by the way she cocked her head to the side that she was trying to hear what the doctor was saying.

"Save one dress to bury her in."

May quickly looked back over at the doctor.

"Oh no!" Patsy screamed.

"Bury her?" May asked, the words barely audible. From the scream, she knew Patsy had heard the doctor as well.

Dr. Peck nodded. His face showed no emotion.

May turned back toward the hall in time to see Patsy crumble down to the floor—the nurse reaching out too late to break the fall— as she fainted.

m

It was late evening when May Ford walked in through the back door and was met with the aroma of chicken, tomatoes, onions, and okra.

"Chicken gumbo?" she asked as she entered the kitchen and saw her husband standing at the stove, large spoon in hand, stirring the contents in the big soup pot.

"Yep," he said as he slowly looked up and over at May.

"This is the second time this week you've had dinner ready when I got home," May said as she sank into a kitchen chair still wearing her coat. She was too weary to smile.

"It's your second time visiting Patsy. I know you're tired coming off of that bus ride. Three hours you've been riding back and forth to Maybury . . ."

May knew that even a year ago, no matter how tired she looked coming off a bus ride, Douglas would not have been standing over the stove when she got home. He couldn't have. He'd have been busy making deliveries or working late into the evening cutting up wood in the driveway on his old donkey saw.

"It's not the bus ride that wears me out," May said to Douglas, closing her eyes. "It's seeing Patsy laying there in that bed. Fifteen minutes they let me see her. And even then she has to turn her head when she talks to me. It's because of the germs, the TB germs, the nurse said. And Patsy's in that drab room. And it's drafty. And the nurses and orderlies come in and out, no one smiles, no one asks her how she's feeling. It's as if they know there's nothing they can do for her. And I can't even hug her, kiss her on the cheek even . . . Oh, Douglas, my heart is so heavy by the time I leave."

"Here May," Douglas said as he put a small bowl of gumbo in front of her. "Have a taste. It's not quite ready, but you need a little something."

"She's only been there two weeks, but it feels like forever," May said as she put the spoon to her mouth. "Lordy," she said, after eating a few mouthfuls, "you haven't lost your touch. It's just like you were still a cook down in one of those big homes in New Orleans!"

"*Chauffeur* cook," he corrected her.

"Goodness, how long has it been?"

"Too long ago to even remember," Douglas said, shaking his head. "It was another life."

"Well, thanks, honey," she said as she pushed the empty bowl away. "I know you're tired too."

May sat there staring at the bowl.

"Three visits a week. That's it. Each family gets to visit three times a week. I'd go there every day if they let me."

"I know you would, but then Patsy wouldn't get the rest she needs. And you'd wear yourself out. Look at you now. You should've seen yourself dragging yourself over to that chair."

"Well Annie's too young to visit—they wouldn't think of letting her in there. And Jean's as thin as a rail—she'd pick up that germ for sure."

"Well either Doug or I will visit over the weekend."

"No, she's my baby! I want to be there for her. I'm her mother! Oh, Douglas, she looks so frail . . . so sad . . ."

The telephone rang. May sat up straight and took a deep breath.

"Probably someone calling to place an order. An evening call at that! Maybe it's a sign business is picking up," she said. The look on Douglas's face told her that he did not hold out much hope for that. Business was slower now in the year after the war. More folks were converting to oil and gas for their furnaces. Gas stoves, too. She knew things would never be the same with the Douglas Ford Wood Company.

The phone was still ringing.

"Are you going to answer that?" Douglas asked.

May turned toward the telephone mounted on the wall behind her and picked up the handset.

"Good evening, Douglas Ford Wood Company," she said, then paused. "Laura? Goodness child, I can barely hear you, speak up, dear . . . What? Say that again, you're whispering, why?" May asked as she turned to face her husband.

She held out her arm and motioned for Douglas to stand closer to her.

"What's she saying?" Douglas asked as he leaned in close to May.

"She said she can't talk louder because the housemother is standing close by, a few feet away, and she doesn't want her to hear," May said, briefly talking away from the mouthpiece.

"Now calm down, child," May said to Laura. She could hear the frantic sound in her daughter's voice.

"You owe what?" May said into the phone. "Oh, dear Jesus," May said, turning again toward Douglas. "Laura got a letter from the university. A bill."

"A bill? For what? She has a scholarship," Douglas said.

"Room and board?" May said, turning her head back to the

phone. Then looking at her husband, she whispered, "It's a bill for her room and board at Stockwell Hall."

"What?" Douglas asked, his voice raised.

"Shhhh! Don't yell! You'll get Laura even more upset . . . Yes, child, I'm here," May said, talking to Laura once again. "So they listed what?" May grabbed the paper and pencil she kept by the phone to write down customer orders for wood. "Keep talking, I'm writing it down . . ."

May cleared her throat and took a deep breath. "Now settle down. Don't let the housemother see you upset. Of course you'll stay in school. No, baby, we'll work it out. No . . . no child. You just focus on your studies. We'll work it out. Now settle down . . ."

"May, what's this all about?"

"No, no, everything will be all right. Send the bill to us. Trust us, baby. Trust God. It will all work out," May said as she tried to make her voice sound calm.

"We love you," she said, "and don't let on to anyone about this bill. This is family business. No one else needs to know, you hear me?"

"May?"

"All right, now, bye-bye." May hung up the phone.

"May? What's this all about?" Douglas asked, looking down at the notes May had scribbled on the paper.

"Oh, Douglas!" she answered, shaking her head slowly, her voice low. "This will break us!"

She watched as her husband sat beside her and stared down at the paper.

"I can barely read what you wrote down here," he said.

"Look, right here," May said, her voice pitching higher as she jabbed at the paper with her finger. "The one line on the bill said tuition, paid in full, University President's Scholars. That's the scholarship Laura was awarded. The next line—look right here—the next line said balance due, room and board, Stockwell Hall . . ."

"Jesus," Douglas said, shaking his head.

"What are we going to do? Business is down, you already let go two of your drivers. Where on earth . . ."

"She'll just have to come home."

"No!" May said firmly. She grabbed the paper in her hand and held it tight. "She will not come home!"

"Wayne University is a fine school."

"She will not come home. We will not lose face like that!"

"Lose face? You're worried about losing face?"

"That's right! Everybody in the neighborhood, at church, her high school classmates, teachers—everybody knows she got a scholarship to that university. We will not lose face bringing her home," May said, her voice shaking.

"Then what do you propose we do?" Douglas asked. "You keep the books, you yourself said this would break us. We aren't bringing in that kind of money anymore."

"I'll get a job," May said, matter-of-factly. She surprised herself as she realized what she had just said. She hadn't had time to think it through; it was as if the words just came out of her mouth on their own.

"And what are you going to do?" her husband asked.

May paused, looking down at the numbers on the paper.

Yes, May Ford, what are you going to do?

"May?" Douglas asked.

If I were home in Clarksville I could teach somewhere—that's what I'd do—at one of the schools for Negro students. I know I could. They'd remember me and all the years I taught at the Clarksville Colored School. All the years. But they do things different up here. Here in Detroit, I'd need to show them my credentials, and I didn't get that certificate. I can't teach up here without that piece of paper. They have some Negro teachers. Oh, I could kick myself for not finishing! Well, I can still work. My mother always worked . . . day work . . . she did cleaning, ironing . . . And I can do it too! I'll—

"May, I said, what are you going to do?" Douglas asked again.

"What?" May said, startled.

"I said what—"

"Why . . . why I'll do day work," May blurted out.

"Day work? You?" Douglas asked. "But you were a teacher down in Clarksville!"

"Well that can't happen up here, can it? Because I didn't finish my program. I was one project away from getting my certificate." She looked over at her husband. "I'll do what I have to do, Douglas. We need the money now."

"But what about the business? Who's going to take the calls?" he asked.

"We aren't getting that many calls for new orders, you know that," she answered. "And our regular customers, I'll write out notes for you to hand out when you make your next deliveries telling them to please call in the evening hours to place their orders. They'll be happy to oblige."

"Day work, May?"

"And why not? It's honest work. My mother did it . . ." May's voice trailed off.

Day work . . . that's what I said all right. And I'll do it, too. I can do it.

May stared at the numbers she had written down on the paper, the amount they owed the university for room and board.

But what would Mama say? She was so proud of me, attending Tennessee A&I, teaching at that colored school. I can hear her now: You've made me proud. And then talking about that judge, You would have made him proud . . . he said he wanted you to be the best a colored woman could be . . .

May paused to collect the thoughts that were whirring through her head.

Mama would still be proud. I have to believe that. Whether it was doing day work or teaching at some school, she'd know I was doing it

for the girls. Because Douglas and I want the same thing for our girls.
Patsy, Laura, Jean, Annie May—they'll be the best a Negro woman
can be. I'll see to it. And I'll see that Laura stays at that university.

"And where will you work?" Douglas asked.

"For goodness' sake," May said, now growing tired of the talk,
"ask some of your customers in Grosse Pointe. Some of them must
be looking for someone to clean, iron . . ."

Douglas shook his head. "Oh, May . . ." he said. He put his
hand on May's arm. "What will the neighbors think? You going
out and doing day work. You've worked the business all these
years . . . And they all know you were a teacher down home."

May pulled her arm away from Douglas and sat up straight.
"And I couldn't care less what those old gossips have to say. Our
children are the ones going to college. Our son's going to be a
doctor. Our girls'll be teachers. Let them talk!"

She leaned in toward her husband. "And I'll still be working
the business, taking the calls, keeping the books. But it's no
secret business is down. The neighbors all know you had to let
Johnson and Katzinger go. Word spread fast through the neighborhood, I know that for a fact. Right after you let those drivers
go, Cleota, Sadie—they came over. 'I heard,' Sadie said. 'I never
thought I'd see the day,' Cleota said to me. Mrs. Rogers stopped
me on the sidewalk. 'Is it true?' she asked. 'You heard right,' I
told all those old gossips. They'll just think I'm helping us out
over a rough patch in the business."

Douglas sighed. "You're going to work yourself to death. The
child should just come home."

"Never in this life will we bring that girl home," May said deliberately. "As far as anyone else needs to know, Laura got a full scholarship to attend the University of Michigan. And I'll do whatever
I have to do to keep her at that school. Whatever."

ᔢ

"Oh, Patsy!" May Ford cried out as she pushed open the double doors and strode into the room at Maybury Sanitarium.

From where she lay on the bed, flat on her back, Patsy turned her head toward the doors. "Mother!" she said, then quickly turned her head away.

"I went to your old room and saw your empty bed!" May placed her hand to her heart. "Scared me to death! I thought . . . well I thought you had . . ." She shook her head. "I ran to the nurses station. The head nurse told me you had been moved here." She stepped closer to the bed. "They should have called and told us. They should've let us know they'd moved you to a different room before I came here and—"

May cut herself off mid-sentence as she looked around the room.

"Goodness knows," she said, "the old room was nothing to speak of, but this one . . ."

May turned and continued to survey the room. Then she shivered.

"This room is drafty. The walls look downright filthy! Worse than the dingy walls in that other room. Why on earth did they move you here?"

Then, remembering that she and Patsy were not alone in the room, May Ford turned and looked at Patsy's roommate, Ora Clark.

"Hello, Ora, I didn't mean to ignore you, dear," May said.

"That's quite all right, Mrs. Ford," Ora said from where she lay on her bed, her face turned away toward the other wall.

"It's just that I was so taken aback with Patsy not in the other room . . ."

"Please, don't apologize, Mrs. Ford."

"But this room, how are you supposed to heal with the draft coming through those windows? Was something wrong with that other room? Why did they move you here?" she asked.

Still turned away from her mother, Patsy answered, "I wasn't looking at much of anything when they first brought me in, so I didn't notice then, but I looked in the other rooms when they wheeled us down the corridor. I could tell Ora and I were the only Negro patients in that ward. You'll see when you walk back out—there're mostly Negroes down here. I could see that when they brought us here."

"Well someone didn't like seeing you down in that other ward, that's for sure. A doctor, a nurse . . . As soon as some new white patients were admitted, they got you out of there," May said.

"I'm going to write my boss, Mr. Wheeler," Ora said. "I'm going to ask him to do something. Either get us back into our old room or get them to fix this one up. He knows people. He can talk to someone," she said.

Ora Clark was the private secretary to the head of the automobile union. She let that be known when May first introduced herself. She had chosen to go to business school instead of enrolling in college. She started in the general secretarial pool and quickly moved up to her current position.

May shook her head. "Race matters," she said. "They never let you forget that. Even in this place where folks are d—" May stopped herself before she could say the word.

"That's all right, Mother. You can say it: where folks are dying. Death is all around us, here. I've gotten used to it in the short time I've been at the san. We hear the orderlies' footsteps as they're pushing the gurneys down the hall, taking the dead to the morgue in the basement. And you can tell that they're wheeling out a dead patient. The orderlies are different when they're doing that. There're not whistling or making small talk when they pass another orderly or a nurse in the hallway. You just hear their footsteps as they push the gurney. I pray I'm not the next one."

"Oh, Patsy, don't even think like that," May said.

"I can't help it!"

May Ford rushed to her daughter's bedside, leaned over, and hugged her.

"Mother, don't, you can't . . ." Patsy said.

"I don't care about their rules! You're my child," she said. May pressed her cheek hard against Patsy's cheek.

Good Lord, this may be the last time I get to touch my child while she's still alive. Who knows when I'll be able to make it back here.

She straightened up.

I need to tell her.

May cleared her throat. She began to speak, keeping her voice low, hoping that Ora could not hear from the other side of the room.

"Baby, I need to tell you something," May began. She explained the situation about the money they owed the university for room and board—and how she had decided to do day work to pay for it.

"Day work?" Patsy said in a low voice, taking the cue from her mother. "But you were a teacher."

"I'll do whatever I have to do for my children."

"But why can't she just come home? She can enroll at Wayne University, just like Doug and me."

At that moment, a nurse walked into the room.

"Ma'am, you're not allowed to stand that close to the patient," the nurse said sharply.

"Yes, well, I was just about to leave," May said without turning her head. Then she whispered to Patsy, "I won't be visiting as much. But I'll write to you as often as I can. And your father will come when he can."

"Ma'am," the nurse said again.

May stepped back. "Goodbye, sweetheart."

"Mother, please don't go just yet," Patsy said, raising her voice.

"No, it's time. They only want us to stay fifteen minutes as it is."

"Please don't go!"

May could hear her daughter fighting back tears as she spoke.

She glanced over at the double doors. The nurse was still standing there.

"I'll be back as soon as I can," May said. Looking over at the other bed, she said, "Goodbye, Ora."

As she turned toward the door, the nurse held it open and May walked out. She didn't notice if Ora said anything to her or not as she left. But she heard Patsy.

"Don't go, Mother!"

Her daughter's voice turned into a wail.

"Don't go!"

May steeled herself as she walked down the corridor: it took all her willpower not to run back to that room and wrap her arms around Patsy.

"Don't go!"

The girl did not stop screaming.

"Don't go!"

May Ford kept walking until she made it out of the sanitarium and down the road to the bus stop, the piercing sound of Patsy's cries still pounding in her head.

"Mama?" Jean asked as May Ford entered the kitchen through the back door and slumped onto a chair next to her daughter at the kitchen table, her schoolbooks spread out in front of her.

"Mama," Jean said as she put her pencil down, "you made it home. Finally!"

"It took an extra hour to get out there. Two hours I was getting on and off of buses, one way—you hear me?" May said as she leaned back and rested her head against the top of the chair. "Lord have mercy, I thought I'd never get there. But I should've known, coming like I was from way over on the east side like that. Grosse Pointe's a long way away. Doesn't seem all that far when I'm just going back and forth to work from home, but going out to Maybury, goodness knows!"

"How's Patsy?"

"She's the same, it seems to me," she answered. "I hadn't been out there to see her since I started working for the Pattersons and the Wilsons. I told your father I might go out there today. It's been a month. And I haven't had the time to visit on weekends, catching up with my own laundry and ironing . . ."

"I could help you with the laundry," Jean said.

"No, you won't," May said firmly. "It'll be a sad day when I can't take care of my own family's laundry. No, you take care of your studies. Enjoy singing in those choirs at church and at school."

May sat up and looked around.

"Where's your father and Annie May? Where's Doug?"

"Annie May's asleep already. Doug's not home yet. Probably still at the library. Daddy, he's making a delivery for the city. The dispatch man from the city called him while we were eating dinner. Daddy said not to go to bed until you got home. That's why I was waiting up for you."

"You poor child," May said, leaning forward to kiss Jean on the cheek. "Well, I'm here, so you can go on to bed now."

Jean started stacking up her books and notebooks.

"But there is one thing you can do for me: run me a nice hot bath," May said as she rested back against the chair. "I just want to relax in a nice hot tub."

"Don't you want some dinner? Daddy left a plate for you in the oven," Jean said.

"No, child. I want to relax in a nice hot tub of water," she said again as she closed her eyes. "At least they finally caulked around those drafty windows in Patsy's room. And they slapped on a fresh coat of paint. Patsy said she's most lonesome at night. She said she misses her own bed. She said, when she gets out, she won't ever complain about sharing a bed with you and Annie May . . ."

May drifted off mid-sentence and fell asleep at the kitchen table.

"Mama?"

May felt Jean gently shaking her.

"Wake up. Your tub's ready."

"Wake up? Good Lord, I fell asleep, didn't I?" May asked, slowly standing up. "Well thank you, sweetheart, for running my tub. Now you go on to bed. Get some rest. You have school tomorrow," she said as she walked past the girls' bedroom, just off the kitchen, and toward the bathroom.

"Good night, baby," she said to Jean as she shut the bathroom door.

May got undressed and sat down in the tub of hot water. She leaned against the back of the tub and felt the water come up to her neck.

Lord have mercy! Jean knows how to run a tub of water. I didn't know hot water could feel so good . . . Lord have mercy . . . just what I needed. I'm so tired.

"May!"

It was Douglas.

"May!"

She felt him shaking her shoulder. Startled awake, but still in a daze, May Ford sat up in the tub. As she moved, water splashed over onto her husband. The entire front of his shirt was wet.

"Jesus Christ, this water's cold! How long have you been lying in this tub of cold water?" Douglas asked.

"Cold? No, Jean ran me a nice hot tub . . ."

Then May fully woke up.

Oh my Lord, what happened . . . this water is ice cold . . .

She looked down at her body, pale—almost stark white—and shivering in the cold water.

"Douglas? Douglas, when did you get home? I asked Jean to run me a hot tub of water . . ."

"Here, let me help you out of this water. You'll catch your death of cold. Here," he said as he reached over and pulled a bath towel from the rod over the tub.

May stood up and Douglas wrapped the towel around her. She could feel herself shivering even under the towel. He rubbed her back and legs. She did not stop shivering.

"Douglas, I'm cold . . . I fell asleep . . . the water . . ."

"We'll get you to bed. I'll pile on the covers."

As they walked toward the kitchen, Douglas rapped hard and loud on the girls' bedroom door.

"Jean! Jean, wake up! Heat up the water in the tea kettle. Fill the hot water bottle," he said as he walked May through the kitchen.

May heard Jean as she opened the bedroom door. "What Daddy? What's going on? Why do you need . . ."

Jean followed them into the dining room. Just as Douglas opened their bedroom door, she asked, "What's wrong with Mama?"

"Never mind about that now, just do as I say. Heat up the water in the tea kettle. Fill the hot water bottle!" he said as he closed the door behind them.

May stood in the middle of their bedroom—still shivering—as her husband raised her arms and pulled her nightgown over her head. As Douglas pulled back the covers, May crawled into the bed and curled up, pulling her knees up to her chest.

"I'm cold, Douglas," she said.

"I know, I know," he said. Douglas opened the door.

"Where's that hot water bottle?"

"The water's not boiling yet," Jean answered.

"Well, just fill it now. Don't wait for the water to boil."

"I'll be fine," May said. "Being in bed here under these covers will warm me up."

"Here, Daddy." It was Jean.

"May, here, hold this up against you."

May hugged the hot water bottle up against her chest. Her

arms felt the warmth. Her breasts felt the warmth. But her legs still shivered.

"What happened, Mama?" Jean asked.

May's voice was weak as she answered, "After you ran that tub of water for me, I must've fallen asleep. Your father came home and found me. The water was ice cold . . . But I'll be fine. I just need to warm up a bit. You go back to bed now."

"Go on now," Douglas said. "She'll be fine come morning."

When May woke up at daybreak, she had stopped shivering. But the coughing fits had started. Her chest hurt.

I must've been coughing all night for my chest to hurt like this.

She shook Douglas.

"Douglas . . . Douglas, wake up. Get the camphor oil and put it in the vaporizer. The steam'll break this cough. I can't go to work coughing like this," she said.

"You aren't going to work," he said as he got out of bed. "I'll call the Wilsons—or is it the Pattersons today?"

"Wilsons," she said. "But it's been barely a month, I can't miss work already."

"I'll call them. You aren't leaving the house today," he said.

Over the next two days, May felt worse and worse. The coughing had turned to hacking fits. The clear mucus she had coughed up was now green.

Doug, Jean, and Annie May all came into her room before leaving for school.

"Stop standing around and staring at me," she said to them, leaning up on her elbow. "I'll be fine. Just go about your business at school," May said.

They each kissed her goodbye. When Doug kissed her forehead, he frowned. "You have a fever," he said. "You didn't have a fever yesterday morning when I kissed you goodbye."

"You aren't a doctor, yet," May said.

"Don't have to be a doctor to feel this fever. You're hot, Mother," Doug said.

With the fever came chills. May was shivering again. Throughout the morning, Douglas piled an extra blanket and a quilt on the bed, but May still shivered under the covers. The camphor oil in the vaporizer did not seem to help. The hot water bottle on her chest did not help.

"I'm calling Dr. Hammonds," Douglas announced.

"You need to get going. You've got deliveries to make," May said.

"I'm not going until Dr. Hammonds sees you," he said.

It wasn't long before Dr. Hammonds arrived. Douglas led him to the bedroom. The doctor put a thermometer under May's tongue.

"One hundred four degrees," the doctor said, squinting at the thermometer. "That's quite a temperature you've got there."

He put the stethoscope to her chest and asked her to take deep breaths. May tried not to cough as she breathed in and out, but she couldn't help herself and exploded into a coughing fit.

"Pneumonia," Dr. Hammonds said as he put the stethoscope back in his black bag.

"Oh, Douglas . . ." May said, looking over at her husband.

Dr. Hammonds patted her on the arm. "Not as contagious as TB, but it can be just as deadly. We caught it early, but you've got to do as I say."

He turned to Douglas Ford; May listened. "She's got to stay flat on her back. Same as they're doing for Patsy out at Maybury. Exact same. Give her lots of hot fluids—broth, strong tea. As long as she's got chills, keep her covered with blankets, quilts, whatever you've got. Those chills'll go away when the fever comes down. But that fever—when it's that high, she may be delirious at some point. If the delirium lasts more than a day, call me. Otherwise, I'll be back to check on her in a few days."

He stood up and looked down at May. "You'll be fine, Mrs. Ford. Just do as I say. Flat on your back."

"I've got to get back to work, Douglas. Help me get dressed," May said as he unbuttoned her nightgown—soaked with sweat—and pulled it over her head.

"That's the fever talking. May, you know you can't work now. Not until this fever breaks and Dr. Hammonds says your lungs are clear."

"I can work. I'm fine . . ."

"Hush, now," he said as he pulled the dry gown over her head. "I paid a call to the Pattersons and the Wilsons. I explained how it is with you. They're decent folks. They both said your job is waiting for you."

"But, I'm fine. I feel fine."

May Ford slumped back against the pillow as her husband tucked the covers in around her shoulders.

"Where are my children? I want to see my children. I don't want to lose another one . . ."

"What are you talking about, May? You haven't lost any children."

"Patsy's gone . . ."

"Patsy's in the sanitarium. Out at Maybury. She's very sick, but she's still alive. You can go out there and see her when you're up and about."

"And Doug, poor Doug . . . the war, killed over in Italy . . . they took my only son. I miss him so much . . ."

"May, come on now. Snap out of it. He's been in each morning before he goes out to Wayne University to kiss you goodbye. The war's over and Doug is home. He's going to medical school just like we planned—Meharry—next fall. He's alive," Douglas said.

"Two of my children, gone . . . it breaks my heart." Tears started flowing down her cheeks.

"You need to get some sleep. You can't keep talking like this. This fever talk will kill you for sure if the pneumonia doesn't." He left the room.

"Douglas! Douglas, come back. Don't leave me. Don't leave me alone!" May cried out.

I'm all alone. Douglas left me all alone. I hear Annie's voice. I hear Jean. He's talking to my girls. Why don't they come here and talk to me? They're all I have left. Jean, Annie—oh, and Laura. I can't forget Laura, away at school like she is . . . I can't forget about her. Yes, he's talking to the girls. I hear him now.

"I talked to Mrs. Rogers from over on Burnside."

He's talking to Annie May and Jean.

"She's coming over tomorrow—Saturday—to start doing the washing and ironing for the family."

Goodness knows, Willa Rogers coming here to do my laundry. I can't have that. I just can't. What will the neighbors think if I can't even do my family's washing and ironing?

"I can do more to help, Daddy!"

That's Jean talking.

"The other night, I washed our blouses and underwear—Annie's and mine—by hand in the sink."

"I know you did, I saw them hanging in the back porch. But this is too much for you girls. I need clean clothes for work, Doug needs his laundry done. And this is more than just our clothes for the week. You see how that pile of sheets in the bathroom has grown. This is real work. Heavy work."

May heard the clink of dishes in the sink while he talked.

"Plus," he said, "I want you both to keep concentrating on your studies. Annie, this is your first year in high school. And Jean, you'll be graduating high school come June. Your educations come first. You both have got plenty to do just keeping up with your schoolwork. No, Mrs. Rogers will be doing our laundry until your mother is back on her feet."

Lord, what's to become of me? I can't even take care of my family. He's bringing in a neighbor woman to do the laundry. What's to become of this family? What's left of us, that is.

May Ford strained to hear.

I can't hear anything. Why aren't they talking? Lord, I'm cold. It feels like I've sweated through this gown already.

May looked up as her husband walked in the bedroom. He was holding a teacup.

"Here you go, May. Mrs. Barker brought this by this morning. She heard you were sick with a fever. She said she brewed it for you fresh this morning. It's a tea. I warmed it up for you. I forget what she says is in it, but she says it'll break your fever. Smells pretty strong. You'll have to hold your nose when you drink it."

Douglas held the cup up to her lips. May pushed it away. Some of the tea spilled onto the quilt.

"What's in that cup, Douglas? It smells like rotten meat! I don't care what she says, I'm not drinking anything that—"

Douglas grabbed May by the jaw and squeezed her mouth open. He quickly poured some of the tea into her mouth.

"There. Now swallow."

May gagged.

"Come on now, or I'll pour some more in."

She swallowed.

"No more, please, no more. That doesn't taste natural. The woman's trying to poison me, for sure. Give me something to get the taste out of my mouth."

As he left the room, May called after him, "Douglas, where're you going? Don't leave me!"

"You said you wanted something to get the taste out of your mouth," he answered.

The woman's trying to kill me for sure. That drink was made from something rotten. I don't know where she . . .

Before her husband could return to the room, May had fallen asleep.

When May opened her eyes, Jean was sitting at the foot of the bed, reading a book.

"Jean, baby, shouldn't you be getting ready to go to school?"

"I went to school already. Classes are done for the day."

"But," May said, "then how . . . you mean I've been asleep all day?"

Jean nodded her head. "Daddy told me to sit here with you until you woke up."

"Bless your heart baby. You and Annie May are all I have left of my children. Laura, I can't forget Laura, too," May said.

"Mama, no. Patsy's alive. She's in the sanitarium. She's going to get better. We'll write a letter to her, and I'll mail it. She'll write back and you'll see she's still alive."

"But Doug, my only son, he's gone . . . buried over in Italy . . ."

"No, Mama, no! Listen to me. Daddy says it's the fever making you talk this way. You have to believe—wait a minute!"

Jean stood up and left the room. She returned quickly with a frame in her hand.

"Don't break my heart, showing me a photograph of my boy," May said, turning her head toward the wall.

"It's not a photograph, Mama. It's a citation."

May did not turn toward Jean.

"Let me read it to you," Jean said. "Doug was a member of the 92nd Infantry, the Negro soldiers. You remember—you told me yourself how they called them the Buffalo Soldiers. Listen Mama, I'm going to read you the citation."

Douglas Ford Jr., Technician Fifth Grade, 317th Medical Battalion, United States Army. For meritorious service in combat on April 5, 1945, in Italy. Technician Fifth Grade Ford was attached to the aid station of an infantry battalion as liaison agent. Feeling that he should be of more service, he volunteered to act as a litter bearer. When the battalion moved out, he took control of a litter squad and led it over Mount Belvedere.

Discovering a wounded man, he administered first aid on the spot and supervised the evacuation. This delay caused the squad to be separated from the rest of the troops. Technician Fifth Grade Ford immediately regrouped his men and, without the aid of maps, led them until he found the aid station the next day. He remained as liaison agent and volunteer litter bearer, supervising the evacuation of casualties, during the entire attack. His example of determination and devotion to duty reflects high credit on the Armed Forces.

By authority contained in Circular Number 73, Headquarters Mediterranean Theater of Operations, you are awarded a Bronze Star Medal.

May stared at her daughter as Jean finished reading the citation. "He's alive? That paper says he's alive?"

"That paper says he returned home a hero, Mother. Your son is a hero," Jean said quietly.

"My son is safe at home. My son is a hero." May repeated Jean's words.

May took her arms out from under the pile of covers. "Hand me that thing," she said to Jean.

Her daughter handed her the framed citation.

May Ford took it, held it up to her face, and read the last line out loud, ". . . you are awarded a Bronze Star Medal."

Then she placed it down against her chest and closed her eyes.

10

1948

DRESS SHOP

Mornings were different in the Ford house. No one, not Jean or her father or Annie May, no one in the family talked about it when they sat down to breakfast almost a year ago. And they did not talk about it now in the summer of 1948. Jean figured it was because they did not want to make their father feel sad. But, no matter. Whether it was then or now, from the moment Jean woke up each day to the familiar aroma of hot oatmeal her mother prepared before leaving for work, she knew what had changed: gone were the sounds of the Douglas Ford Wood Company.

Even before she was tall enough to peer out of the kitchen window, Jean had grown accustomed to the early morning noise of the family business—her father's drivers arriving for work and, one by one, revving up the engines of the trucks that were parked on the driveway along the side of the house. She heard the men who owned their own trucks as they made their way down Halleck Street, riding over the wood planks her father had laid on the street so that their wheels wouldn't get caught in the deep ruts of a gravel road.

She was used to her father rushing about, in and out the back door, calling out, "Where're the rest of my drivers? Katzinger? Jones? Good Lord, those men are gonna be the death of me! How can I run a business . . ."

Then, when Jean was old enough to push the chair up beneath the window and climb up to peek out into the wood yard, she appointed herself the lookout and would announce to her father, "Mr. Jones just walked up, Daddy. I see Mr. Katz, he's running up the driveway, too!"

And the telephone. Early in the morning, the calls would start coming in. When the phone rang, Jean and the other children knew that all chatter at the breakfast table was expected to stop. When Annie May was still little, Doug or one of Jean's older sisters—as if on cue—grabbed the baby and took her into the girls' bedroom in case she started to cry. With the children quiet and the baby gone, then and only then would their mother pick up the handset from its perch on the kitchen wall.

"Douglas Ford Wood Company," May Ford would say. "Yes, good morning, Mr. Barnes. Yes, a cord of wood, delivered tomorrow evening. Yes, thank you. Indeed . . ."

The noise of that saw, the *hee haw, hee haw* of the donkey saw—even before his drivers arrived, Jean watched her father out in the wood yard standing at the blade and cutting up what was left of the loads of wood from the day before. Then, when the crew was all there, he and the drivers left for the automobile factories. He had told her many a time how they took crowbars and broke apart the wooden crates that the car parts were delivered in. They loaded the flatbeds of the trucks and brought the pieces of wood back to the wood yard where he would cut them up into firewood.

"Our customers use it just like we do," he told Jean once, as she stood off to the side, watching him work the saw. "They'll feed the firewood into a big cast-iron stove in the kitchen for cooking or in the other rooms to keep the house warm."

Then there was the other part of the business: For as long as she could remember, Jean watched as her mother kept records of the orders in an old leather-bound ledger. She wrote down the customer's name, address, how much wood in the order, and the amount owed, each in a separate column. Her father then took that ledger and wrote notes on slips of paper that he passed out to his drivers as they headed back to the trucks, telling them where to go, how much wood to deliver, and how much money to collect.

Hee haw, hee haw. The sound of the donkey saw never seemed to end, until it did.

Now when Jean peered out the kitchen window, she was a young woman going into her sophomore year in college. And the donkey saw was gone. She shook her head at the thought of it.

Almost a year ago . . . the fall of 1947. That's when it happened, about a year after Laura left for the university in Ann Arbor and Patsy went to the sanitarium. The year after Mama started day work and came down with pneumonia. Doug was in his first year of medical school—Meharry, down in Nashville. I'd just started my freshman classes down at Wayne University. Things changed in the family. Things changed for the business. And the business seemed to change really fast.

Where are you going, Douglas? Mama asked as Daddy walked out the back door.

Got something to do, May, he said.

Then I watched—from right here at the kitchen window—as Daddy picked up a crowbar and proceeded to take apart that old donkey saw of his. By then Mama was standing behind me watching him, too. Annie came out of the bedroom.

What's going on? What's that noise? she asked.

Shhh! Mama said. Lord knows he tried to get a loan, she said as she stood there with us. We all watched until Mama said she couldn't watch anymore and left the kitchen.

Jean took in a deep breath and slowly let it out.

Mama said many a time that getting pneumonia knocked the wind out of her for the longest. Said even now it's all she can do sometimes to put one foot in front of the other and walk out of the house and over to the bus stop. But I think Daddy closing the business was worse on her. She never said it, but I know it left a big hole in her life—no more keeping the books, no more answering all those phone calls and taking down orders.

"Why, Daddy?" Jean had asked her father that same evening a year ago as he sat in the living room after dinner and packed tobacco into the bowl of his pipe.

During dinner, Douglas Ford had announced that he had let go the last of his drivers, Mr. Jones.

"Other than taking down that donkey saw, it was one of the hardest things I've ever had to do"—he pressed down on the tobacco—"him being a family friend and all. But the war's over, and folks are ready to modernize. Can't stop progress," he said.

"You did the best you could," Mama had said as she walked into the living room.

Her father gripped the pipe's bit with his teeth as he talked. "All those years with the wood business, my fleet of trucks, a ledger full of orders . . . none of that meant a hill of beans to those white fellas at the banks. I even came with references from some of my long-time customers, white folks from Grosse Pointe. Family names I know they recognized. Didn't matter. Every last one of those bank fellas, they just shook their heads and pushed the papers back at me." He leaned forward. "I had my business plan. I was going to convert from wood deliveries to oil. Folks are getting furnaces and are heating with oil now. I understand that. I just needed a loan to buy my first tanker. With the profits from that, I could buy another and another, hire some of my drivers back. I had the plan laid out. Humph! It was a waste of time. A waste of time for a Negro to walk in there and try to talk business to those fellas."

"Don't be so hard on yourself, baby," Mama had said, sitting on the sofa with her sewing basket in her lap.

"May, you know it's true. Well, no matter. Got as good a deal as I'm gonna get for those trucks, leasing them to the city. City's paying me decent money. The ice man told me he tried to lease his truck to the city, what with just about everybody having a Frigidaire now, but they wouldn't take it. Glad I kept mine in good running order."

He stopped, closed his eyes, and took a few puffs of his pipe. "And I went over to Long Manufacturing this afternoon. Talked to the plant manager over there—"

"Oh, Douglas, why didn't you tell me?" Mama interrupted.

"It was just this afternoon, May, that I talked to the fella," Daddy had answered. "Anyways, he says I can start work there anytime I want. You'll see, it'll work out for the best. I can walk to work."

Now—just a year later—fruit trees have taken root where the wood yard used to be. Where the wood used to be piled high, almost as high as the roof of our house. Daddy cleared the debris and planted fruit trees: peach, cherry, pear, apple. He said, Once they start bearing fruit, your mother can put it up in the summer. Especially since the fruit peddlers don't come by like they used to.

Jean sighed to herself as she turned away from the window.

Next, Daddy bought a furnace, had it installed in the cellar, and started heating the house with oil. Put what he calls baseboard registers in every room to heat the house.

She looked around the kitchen.

Got a gas stove, too. Good Lord, Daddy was right. You can't stop progress.

It was late in the summer of 1948, after Labor Day. Annie May was entering her junior year in high school, and Jean was starting her sophomore year at Wayne University. Laura was still at the University of Michigan, going into her junior year. Doug was back in Nashville, entering his second year at Meharry. And Patsy was only now home from the sanitarium. The TB was gone; her lungs were clear.

It seemed to Jean that every time her mother looked over at Patsy, she would shake her head in disbelief and say, "Courting in the sanitarium, have mercy, whoever heard of such a thing?" or "It's a miracle that girl is still alive. It's just a miracle my baby's home." Or "Good Lord, it's a miracle! And now that boy has come and asked your father for your hand in marriage already!"

Patsy walked out of the bedroom and into the kitchen, holding up a set of films. "Look! Jean, Mother, Annie May, come look at these X-rays," Patsy said. May Ford was stirring a pot at the stove. Jean and Annie May were sitting at the kitchen table, snapping a pile of string beans into a bowl. Jean could hear the joy in her sister's voice.

"I called my advisor at the College of Education, this morning. He told me to take them to the university health center. Once they pass inspection, he said he'll sign the papers for me to start my student teaching."

"Bring them closer, let me see," Jean said to Patsy.

"See, there used to be spots here and here," Patsy said, pointing to the image of her lungs.

"Over here," May said from the stove, turning away from the pot. "Show me what you're talking about."

Douglas Ford came into the kitchen. Putting on his reading classes, he said, "Let me have a look at those films."

Jean watched as he studied the X-rays and then looked over at Patsy. "Even though I gave that young man, Mr. Taylor—"

"Bill," Patsy interrupted.

"I told Mr. Taylor he had my permission to marry you, but I reminded him how sick you'd been. I told him to be mindful of that and not rush into this marriage."

"He understands, Daddy," Patsy said softly. Then Patsy turned to her sister. "C'mon, Jean! Come with me to the bridal salon tomorrow. I want someone with me when I order my dress."

"Patsy, it's only September!" Jean answered. "You're getting married next year in June. What's the rush?"

"June will be here before we know it, that's what's the rush! Plus, it takes time to make the gown, and I'll need them to make the bridesmaids' dresses," Patsy explained.

"She's right, Jean," her mother said.

"I've got the sketch already drawn—"

"Sketch?" Annie May interrupted.

"Mother said I could design my own gown."

"May?" her father asked as he looked over at his wife.

"Don't worry, Douglas," her mother said. "I told her we'd only spend up to fifty dollars. Anything over that she'd have to pay."

Jean watched as her parents both looked over at Patsy.

May asked, "You remember me saying that, don't you Patsy?"

"Yes, Mother, I remember. I have my savings. I can add some of that to the fifty."

Jean wasn't surprised to hear Patsy bring up her savings. Each of the five Ford children had been required to maintain a savings account with the post office. It was their mother's immutable rule: if any money came into their hands, a portion had to be saved. And Patsy had worked several jobs before she got sick. Jean had a bit of money put away from giving piano lessons and working the concession stand over on Belle Isle during the war.

"Well, don't spend all of your savings on that dress," May said.

"May, she can spend her money as she sees fit," Douglas said.

"I know, Douglas, but I'm just saying . . ." She turned back toward the stove. "Just don't spend it all."

The next morning, Jean walked over to Hamtramck with Patsy to the Kelly Bridal Shop in the shopping district on Joseph Campau Street, near their home. Patsy stood at the shop's counter with her sketch in hand and described to the clerk the dress that she wanted. While Patsy talked to the clerk, Jean studied the gowns hanging on a nearby rack.

I don't care what she says, it's still early to be ordering a gown for a June wedding.

Jean pulled a gown from the rack and held it out in front of her. "This is beautiful," Jean murmured.

"What did you say?" Patsy asked from the counter.

"Nothing. Just looking over here," Jean answered. She put the dress back on the rack.

I know Patsy's not the only one. It seems like that's what so many couples are doing now that the war is over. They seem to be in such a hurry to get married. You can't sit down to lunch over in Old Main without hearing talk of so-and-so getting engaged or making wedding plans . . . I guess they're getting on with their lives but still.

"Just a minute, I'll have to get the owner," Jean heard the clerk say. She looked over to the counter in time to see the clerk take the drawing and disappear into a back room. A moment later, the clerk emerged with a woman she introduced as the owner of the shop. She was a short, middle-aged woman who spoke with a heavy Polish accent. She talked like she was from the old country, her mother would say.

"Young lady," she said while peering at Patsy above the rim of her reading glasses. "You have designed a very beautiful dress and veil, here."

Jean knew the design. Patsy had outlined a gown, fitted at the waist with a side swirling skirt. The long sleeves as well as the bodice above the bust were lace. A mantilla veil cascaded from an upright headpiece.

Could Patsy have designed an uglier headpiece? It sticks straight up, like she's got a fan on the top of her head! Well, it's her wedding and if that's how she wants to look . . . I'm not the one wearing it, so it doesn't matter what I think about it.

"What fabric did you have in mind?" the owner asked.

"Silk," Patsy replied confidently. "And lace for the veil."

"Of course," the owner replied. She continued, "This dress will cost you one hundred and twenty-five dollars."

Jean almost gasped.

That woman has lost her mind! One hundred and twenty-five?

Jean looked over at Patsy. Her sister's facial expression did not change.

"If you bring in a fifty-dollar deposit, I will then take your measurements." The owner stepped back and took in Patsy's entire frame. "You are such a thin child, my dear."

"I'll bring the fifty dollars to you next week," Patsy said, nodding.

Now I've heard everything—Patsy has lost her mind as well!

Jean followed Patsy as she made a move toward the door.

As soon as they walked out of the shop, Jean grabbed Patsy's elbow. "Patsy, how—"

"Shhh!" Patsy said.

They walked a few steps away from the salon. Then, when they were safely out of hearing range, Jean stopped, grabbed her sister by the elbow and asked, "You're going to pay that much for the gown?"

"It's the one I want," Patsy replied defensively. "Come on, let's keep walking."

"But that's so much money!"

"Jean, I dreamed about that dress while I was flat on my back out at Maybury after Bill started talking marriage and us having a future together." They stopped walking, and Patsy looked her sister straight in the eye. "I told myself that if I lived to get out of that place—and if Bill would still have me—I would be married in a dress like that. It's the gown of my dreams, and I intend to get married in that dress!"

"But, Patsy . . ." Jean said.

"Come on," Patsy said. "The ice cream parlor's just up ahead."

When they reached the door of the ice cream shop, Patsy said, "This is another thing I promised myself."

"Ice cream?"

"Yes! I promised myself that if I left that place alive, I'd have ice cream every day if I wanted it."

They stopped talking as they stepped inside and surveyed the room. The stools at the counter were all taken.

"Let's sit over there," Jean said, pointing toward an empty booth. Jean continued the conversation.

"But ice cream every day? Patsy, you can't—"

"No, you don't understand. I know you can't have ice cream every day. But the food there, it was so terrible. I don't think they wanted to spend much money on meals for patients they didn't expect to live from one day to the next."

"Patsy, don't say that!"

"It's true! Death was all around us. I knew it. We all knew it. And that's why I'm sure they fed us like we were going to die. They gave us a slice of bread, mashed potatoes, boiled meat—half the time you couldn't even tell what kind of meat it was. The thought of ice cream when I got out of there—it was just a game I played. It seemed to make the food taste better. Don't ask me how, but it did," Patsy said. Then she leaned forward. "Anything to take my mind off that place. That's why it meant so much to me when Bill would visit. It was another thing that gave me hope, a reason to live. It would get so god-awful lonely out there. And when Mama stopped visiting for the longest time . . . I know it was because of the day work and all, but I was so lonely. So to hear the sound of Bill's motorcycle coming up the road, getting louder as he got closer to the gate—"

Jean chuckled. "Remember, right before you got sick, when Mama told him to turn off the engine to his motorcycle before he turned onto Halleck, while he was still on Dequindre, and to walk it up the street to our house? Told him he was disturbing the quiet of the neighborhood?" Jean laughed out loud.

"And he did it, too," Patsy said, laughing with Jean. "Walked it all the way to the driveway!"

"I think he was afraid to cross Mama," Jean said, still laughing.

Then Jean stopped laughing. She thought about what Patsy had just said, about being lonely and how Mama had stopped visiting.

She's home now. She's all better. She needs to know. She needs to know the real reason Mama stopped visiting.

"You know why Mama stopped visiting for that long spell, don't you?"

"She said she was going to start day work to pay for Laura's room and board at the University of Michigan."

"You want to know the real reason?" Jean asked.

"Real reason? What do you mean?" Patsy asked.

"She caught pneumonia," Jean said flatly.

"What?"

Jean told Patsy about their mother falling asleep in the bathtub that night.

"When Daddy got home and woke her up, Mama was sitting in a tub of cold water. Chilled to the bone, she said she was. Wasn't long after that she got sick."

Jean paused. Patsy was looking at her, her mouth almost hanging open.

Right then a waitress came over to their booth and asked, "What can I get you today?"

Patsy was still staring at Jean. Jean answered for both of them. "Two ice cream sundaes, vanilla ice cream, hot fudge, whipped cream, and a cherry on top."

"Right away," the waitress said.

"Mama had a terrible fever," Jean continued, talking fast. "She was delirious. She was talking all out of her head. She thought Doug had died over in Italy."

"Died? What?"

"Then she was talking about Clarksville, too. About her father. You know she doesn't talk about him much, but when she does, she always calls him Mr. Jackson. Well, she said something she'd never said before, at least not to me. She said Mr. Jackson wasn't her father. Said it over and over when I was sitting there with her during the worst of the fever. Then she didn't bring it up again once the fever broke."

There was silence for a moment.

Oh Lord, what was I thinking? Why did I tell Patsy what Mama said about Grandpa Jackson? Maybe Patsy doesn't know. Maybe Mama doesn't want her to know.

"Grandpa Jackson *isn't* her father," Patsy said.

There you go. She knows. Good God, she knows, too.

"Come on now, I know you figured it out by yourself, even before Mama said what she said to you with that fever talk." They looked each other straight in the eye.

Patsy continued. "Her daddy was some white man. Who knows who. But it wasn't Grandpa Jackson."

Just then, the waitress came and put the sundaes down in front of them.

"Thank you," Jean said to the woman as she turned to walk away. Jean picked up her spoon, then she looked back at Patsy. "Who said something to you?"

"No one told me."

"Did Mama tell you?" Jean asked.

"No, of course not! I told you, no one told me. No one had to tell me. Thinking about our family, I just figured it out. Mama's color being so bright, as she likes to say. And then her brother, Uncle Willie. You probably don't remember seeing him when we'd visit down in Clarksville . . ."

Jean shook her head. "No I don't. I was too young before he died."

"Well, I remember him, and he was dark like our Daddy is. And you know Grandma Jackson was brown skinned, not as dark as Uncle Willie, but she was brown."

Jean nodded her head. "I remember."

"Now Mama, Aunt Patsy, Aunt Addie—all the sisters came out bright, almost white. And Uncle Willie, he was the youngest. He was the only dark one. Grandpa Jackson was Willie's father, that's for sure. But the girls—Mama and the sisters—their daddy was white."

Jean took a deep breath and slowly let it out.

What do I say?

"So who told *you*?" Patsy asked. "Come on . . . stop acting like you didn't know."

Jean paused.

God, I haven't thought about that afternoon when Raylene Wilson came by the house in a long, long time. I might as well tell her. Don't know why I never told her about it before. Never told her, Laura . . . Annie neither. We just never talked about it. Mama's bright. We're brown, and that's how it is.

"Jean?" Patsy asked.

"Raylene Wilson," Jean said.

"Who?" Patsy asked. "You mean that woman from over on Burnside?"

"Goddard," Jean said.

"Yeah, right, Goddard Street. She and her family were from Alabama if I remember. They moved in the neighborhood after most other folks were long ago settled in. And her head twitched. Like she couldn't stop it."

"Yeah, that's her," Jean said. "I was ten years old, and I remember I was ten because that was the summer I lost my stutter, just like Grandma Jackson said I would. I heard her and Mama talking once when we went down there to visit after that big flood. She told Mama I would lose my stutter when I got older."

"Um-hum, I remember going down there after that flood. The big flood of 1937 they called it. And that's the summer Grandma Jackson taught me to quilt. We never saw her again, either," Patsy said. "She died that winter, two days after Christmas. I wanted to go down to the funeral with Mama, but she said it was best if I stayed home to help Daddy look after you girls."

Jean said, "Well then you remember how Mama used to make us polish the silver every Sunday."

"Lordy, don't I remember!" Patsy said.

For as long as Jean could remember, her father insisted that the family sit down to a formal dinner in the dining room each Sunday afternoon and use the sterling silver service he had bought down in New Orleans: flatware, platters, serving bowls, chafing dish, a tea pot, and sugar bowl. Her mother ironed a linen tablecloth on Saturday nights and spread it across the dining room table. Then she laid out the silver pieces they would need for the Sunday meal. When the girls were old enough, it was their job to polish the silver after they came home from church.

"I hated that job!" Patsy added.

"It wasn't so bad," Jean said.

"That's because you were younger. Mama had to go back over the pieces you polished," Patsy said.

"No, really? I never saw her do that!"

"Well she did. Daddy wanted each piece to be like a mirror. That's what Mama said. He wanted to be able to see himself in the silver when he walked by the china cabinet. She said that rich widow he chauffeured down in New Orleans kept her silver polished like that."

"Not just a chauffeur," Jean said. "He was a cook for that widow, too."

"You're right, you're right. But still, that silver had to shine!" Patsy said.

"I remember Laura used to spit—" but before Jean could finish her sentence, Patsy cut her off.

"Wait a minute, what's all this got to do with Raylene Wilson?" Patsy asked.

"Well, I'm about to tell you!" Jean said. She stuck her spoon into the top of her ice cream sundae and leaned in against the table.

"It was a Sunday evening after dinner. We had eaten and us girls helped Mama do the dishes, and she had put all the silver pieces back in the china cabinet. I don't remember any neighbors stopping by that evening. You know how they would do on a Sunday, stop by for a dish of ice cream or to use the telephone or whatever, but not that day. Anyway, Daddy and Doug had gone somewhere in the truck. You and Laura and Annie were out in the backyard. You were probably working on one of your quilts. I could hear Laura and Annie May out on the driveway beside the house playing jump rope, reciting that singsong rhyme, remember the one we used to say—'Who stole the cookie from the cookie jar? Number one stole the cookie from the cookie jar. Who me? Yes, you. Couldn't be! Then who? Number two stole the cookie from the cookie jar.'"

Patsy nodded and smiled. "I remember that silly song."

"I had stayed back in the kitchen with Mama. I was reading a book at the kitchen table and Mama had her fountain pen and jar of ink and some of that linen stationery she likes to use. Even today she still buys a box of it whenever we pass the stationery counter at Klein's or wherever. Anyway, she was writing a letter to one of her Clarksville friends, probably. Then there was a knock at the front door. I could see straight to the screen door from where I was sitting in the kitchen that there was a woman standing there. She was peering into the living room through the screen, and I knew right away it was Raylene Wilson before Mama even said a word. I could tell by the head twitching."

Mama said, Who is that knocking at the front door? Folks around here know to come around to the back door. Lord have mercy . . .

I watched Mama get up from the table and go up to the screen door—Why Mrs. Wilson, good evening, she said. How are you? I wasn't expecting you.

I know, I know, forgive me for coming out of the blue like this, Raylene said to Mama, but I wanted to thank you for the jars of food you sent over the other day. That was mighty generous of you.

Patsy was steadily eating her sundae while Jean talked. Jean stopped talking for a minute and ate a few spoons of whipped cream and ice cream. Then she put her spoon back in the dish.

"Why don't you finish your sundae?" Patsy asked. "You can tell me about Raylene later."

"No, I want you to hear what I have to say all in one piece. So listen, a few days before, maybe a week, I don't really remember, Mama had sent Laura and me over to the Wilson house with some jars of string beans, corn, and tomatoes. Stuff like that. She hadn't yet finished putting up the rest of those thousand jars she canned for the family every summer. But she said she had heard that the Wilsons were going through a rough time since moving up here. Mama said she had plenty to share. You know how she always helped folks out like that."

Anyway, Raylene was standing at the door and Mama said something like, Glad to share what we have, Mrs. Wilson, won't you come in for a bit?

Mama unlatched the door to let the woman in, and as soon as Raylene stepped into the living room, I could see her eyes get all big and wide. She looked all around the room.

Mrs. Ford . . . Mrs. Ford you sure do have a lovely home, she said to Mama. Mama thanked her and said, Let's just go on back to the kitchen. And then as Mama led Raylene into the dining room, I could see the woman stop in front of the china cabinet. She put her hand up to her mouth and then she said, Lord have mercy, I can see myself in all that silver. Look at that—just like a mirror! I didn't know colored folks had anything this nice, she said. Never in my life . . . Her head twitched even faster as she leaned in closer to the cabinet. Mrs. Wilson? Mama said to her. Just follow me into the kitchen . . .

I could see how Raylene's face had changed after looking at those silver pieces. She got a scrunched up look about her. Almost a mean look. And her head was twitching up a storm. When she walked into the kitchen, she looked straight at me but didn't say a word. I moved over to the stool next to the stove and sat there. Mama motioned for Raylene to take a seat at the kitchen table. Raylene shook her head.

No, no I can't stay. I just wanted to come by and thank you for the jars, Raylene said. The words were polite enough, but now her tone of voice was cold.

You're most welcome, Mama said. Then Raylene said, Some of the women said that your husband runs a trucking business.

Yes, that's right. The Douglas Ford Wood Company.

They said he has his own drivers.

Yes, Mr. Ford hires his drivers from the men in the neighborhood, Mama said.

My Harry's good with a tractor. I know he'd be good with a truck. Could you ask your husband if he could hire him to drive one of his trucks?

Well, Mrs. Wilson, Mama answered, he doesn't need any drivers right now.

I don't want to know what you think, Raylene Wilson said, her words short and clipped. I want to hear it from your husband.

Excuse me? Mama asked. You're mistaken if you think you can come into my home and—

And what? You think just because you have light skin and straight hair that you can talk down to me? Raylene said, her voice was getting pretty loud. Living here with all that nice furniture and all that silver, just like a white person, she said. Her right shoulder was twitching now along with her head.

Mrs. Wilson, please don't talk that way in front of my daughter.

I can say what I want, Mrs. Ford.

Not in my house, you can't! Mama said, raising her voice.

You think that just 'cause you look white . . .

Mrs. Wilson, I think it's time for you to leave.

I'll g-g-go when I'm g-good and ready, Raylene said, her head twitching so bad she could barely get the words out. Mama reached back and grabbed the poker that was laying on the stove. You do not come into my house and talk like that, especially in front of my daughter! she said, holding the poker at her side.

Oh yes I can! And I can say what anybody looking at you can see plain as day—that some white man took your mother, that—But before Raylene could finish her sentence, Mama stepped forward quickly, raised the poker above her head and whacked it across the kitchen table, right next to Raylene. Raylene screamed. I screamed.

Now you get out of my house before I let this poker fall across your head, Mama said in a low voice. Patsy, Lord have mercy—I don't think I'd ever seen Mama that angry before. Ever!

Oh Lordy, don't kill me, was all Raylene said. Why she even stopped twitching after Mama hit that poker across the table.

And you leave out the back door, the same door you should have come through to begin with, Mama said. Raylene ran out of kitchen and through the back door. Mama followed close behind, the poker still in her hand.

Help! Help! I'll call the police! Raylene said.

Go on and call the police, but first you get off my property! I heard Mama say to her.

Then Patsy said to Jean, "I do remember! Yes, I remember hearing the screams, looking up and seeing Mama come running out the back door with that poker in her hand. Walking fast, close behind Raylene, telling her to get off of our property. I remember that now. Annie and Laura stopped jumping. I looked up from my quilting. Raylene ran off down the driveway and Mama stood by the porch and watched her go. Didn't say a word. Then she turned and went back into the house, like nothing had happened. So I just went back to my quilting. The girls started jumping rope again . . . Funny how the mind works. I never thought about it, not until just now."

"Well, when Mama came back into the kitchen, I was still sitting on the stool. 'That woman has lost her natural mind,' she said to me. Her voice was calm again. 'Just go back to doing what you were doing. Read your book. Everything's all right. That woman's gone now. She's not thinking straight, is all, and she said some things that ought not be said. That's why I had to ask her to leave our house. She won't be coming back here. You can be sure of that.'"

Jean looked at Patsy and leaned back against her chair. "And Mama never said another word about what happened that day. Never. But Raylene's words—some white man took your mother—they stuck with me. I guess because when Raylene said what she said, that's when Mama whacked the poker across the table. Scared me to death! I didn't know what those words meant. And that poker left a mark on the table, even though I could tell Mama or maybe Daddy tried to smooth it out sometime after that. But I could still tell where that mark had been. And sometimes when I looked at it, I remembered what Raylene said. Wasn't until I got older and learned about the way of things, you know, between a man and a woman, that I understood what Raylene meant and why Mama got so angry. What it all meant about Mama's color and Grandma Jackson."

Patsy shook her head. "Well, that's the South for you," she said. "And back then, there was nothing a Negro woman could do about it. Or her husband, for that matter, if she was married. Didn't really matter if the woman was married or not. If a white man took a fancy to a Negro woman, well it was as simple as that! If anybody said a thing, any Negro that is, they'd be lynched. Strung up on a tree!" Patsy said. "And you know I'm telling the truth."

Jean said, "I wish it wasn't true, but you look at Mama, her sisters, and you know that's how it was."

"That's how it's been for a whole lot of Negro women," Patsy said. "Truth is, I don't know if things have changed very much down there, down South, even now."

Jean let out a sigh. "I wonder if Mama knows who her daddy was—her white daddy?"

Patsy shrugged her shoulders.

"I know I'll never ask her, I know that much," Jean said.

"Me neither," Patsy said.

Goodness knows, Grandma Jackson's probably turning over in her grave listening to what we've been saying about her and Mama and . . .

Patsy said, "Well, enough of that talk. Look at you, you've barely touched your sundae. Go on and finish."

"Oh, goodness Lord, look at this," Jean said, looking down in front of her as she picked up her spoon. "What a mess on the table!"

Chocolate sauce was swirling around a pool of melted vanilla ice cream that had spilled over the edge of the dish.

Jean ate the cherry that had slid from the top of the sundae and was resting against the side of the bowl. Then she dug in her spoon and started to eat the rest.

11

1949

RECREATION CENTER

It had been a long time since Jean Ford last thought about what happened that night. In fact, until the memories came roaring back five years later at the Cardoni Recreation Center, she could not remember exactly when the last time was that she had even thought about it.

The year was 1944, and Jean wanted to do something—anything—that would make it feel like she was helping with the war effort. Everyone was doing something extra. And even though at the age of fifteen she was not legally old enough to do so, she asked her father to let her take a job at one of the concession stands at Belle Isle, a popular island park in the middle of the Detroit River. And though a job at a concession stand, where she would be working evenings and getting home after dark, was not even remotely connected with the war effort, she persuaded him to let her take the job. The supervisor doing the hiring didn't seem to care how old she was, as long as she promised to show up on time and not steal money from the cash register.

It had happened the night she decided to save her dime. Instead of spending it on the bus that went around the island and then across the bridge to the bay where she caught another bus that took her home, Jean decided to take a shortcut through the woods. She had noticed the path more than once while sitting on the bus after work. She could tell that many folks had used it before her because it was a well-worn path, the grass trampled down so far that it was mostly dirt under foot.

Jean had just wanted to block out any memory of what had happened: of that man, of falling in the mud, of the bus ride home, of her mother's scream, and her father's fury. And she had pretty much done so. She had not had a flashback to that night, when she was a foolhardy fifteen-year-old, until several years later, on a Thursday evening at the recreation center.

∞

It was the summer of 1948, and Jean had finished her freshman year at Wayne University. She had one year left in a two-year merit scholarship that paid all of her tuition through the end of her sophomore year. She wanted to work and earn as much as she could over the summer to add to her savings for junior and senior year tuition and to supplement what her parents had been set-ting aside over the years. Jean applied for a part-time job with the city of Detroit's Recreation Department, where most of the other Negro students at the university worked, some even full-time, while they studied for their degrees. She applied, got hired, and was assigned to the Cardoni Center, located at Oakland and Dequindre. While it was just two short bus rides from the center to her home, her neighborhood and the one surrounding Cardoni were worlds apart.

Mr. Morgan, her supervisor, noted as much when he looked at her paperwork on her first day there.

"Miss Ford, you live on Halleck Street? Off of Dequindre?" he asked as he sat behind a desk that took up most of the space in his small office. He was a dark-skinned, heavyset man with a deep voice.

Jean nodded.

"I know that area. This area around here's different. Very different. Think you can handle it?" he asked her.

Jean's neighborhood was unusual for Detroit, with its mixture of Eastern European immigrants and Negroes who had migrated from the South. The residents who lived near the Cardoni Center were Negro. Jean's community was quiet and very stable. The neighborhood surrounding the Cardoni Center was considered a rough and dangerous part of the city. The residents there saw few of the city services Jean was accustomed to, like repairing sidewalks and replacing streetlights. There were few police patrols. Jean knew the difference because during lunch on campus, in the basement cafeteria at Old Main, her friends at the university made sure she knew the way of it after she told them where she had been assigned. They warned her to be careful and watch herself.

"Yes, Mr. Morgan. I can handle it," Jean answered.

He closed her folder, leaned forward and spoke. "This recreation center is city property. The playground, too. No crap games, no alcohol, no prostitution . . ."

Jean flinched at that last word. She could tell Mr. Morgan noticed.

"Yes, I said prostitution. You see the girls hanging out in the bathroom, you tell them they've got to go. Those girls come on Thursdays when there's square dancing. You tell them there's no hanging out in the bathroom, no hanging around the doorways. You tell them to get out on the dance floor."

"I will, Mr. Morgan," Jean said.

"You see a weapon on the playground—a knife, a gun—you gather up your kids and you bring them inside. Then you call the police right away."

Jean was silent. She knew she must have looked frightened because of what Mr. Morgan said next.

"I'm not trying to scare you," he said. "That's just how it is around here. But if you take care of the little problems, things won't get out of hand."

That first year, Mr. Morgan had Jean assist one of the captains—the title he gave the experienced university students who worked there. There were four in total, all Negroes. He assigned each captain to work with a group of youth that he had divided by age and gender.

At the end of the summer, Mr. Morgan called Jean into his office.

"You've done well," he began. "You learned from your captain. And you have a nice way with the children."

"Thank you, Mr. Morgan," Jean said.

"Next summer, you'll be a captain yourself," he said. "In the meantime, when your classes start back in, you can work as many hours here as you'd like—evenings, weekends, you just let me know."

"Thank you, Mr. Morgan," she said again. "Weekends are best for me. I'm either at the library or teaching piano lessons most evenings during the week. Weekends are better."

In the summer of 1949, Mr. Morgan kept his word and made Jean a captain. She was responsible for supervising the younger girls and their playground games. When it got too hot to play outdoors, she brought the girls inside and had them work on craft projects—pinwheels tacked to pencils, finger puppets made from felt, flowers folded from crepe paper—to keep them occupied until it was time for them to go home.

Jean was leading a group of girls in a game of dodgeball one afternoon when she noticed two white police officers in a patrol car cruising the streets around the playground. She saw the car stop and was surprised when the officer on the passenger side leaned his head out of the window and told her to come over to the car.

"Keep the ball m-m-m-moving," she said to the girls. "I'll be right back."

Jean noticed the shocked look on the girls' faces, and she knew why they looked at her that way. That was the first time she had stuttered since she started working at Cardoni. The first time she had stuttered in quite a long while. The stutter seemed to go away when she was ten years old, but it did come back when she was nervous or anxious—like when the policeman ordered her over to his patrol car.

"Excuse me, young lady," he called out. "Excuse me—over here!" He stretched his arm out of the window and motioned with his finger for Jean to come over to the car.

Jean walked to the police car.

"You been working here long?" the policeman asked her.

"Since last summer," she answered.

"We're looking for a young Negro man," he said. "Looks to be twenty years old, about your color, a gold front tooth. He walks with a slight limp. You seen anyone fits that description?" he asked.

"No . . . no, I d-d-don't think so," Jean answered. "What's he d-done?"

"We just want to ask him a few questions," the officer responded. "We'll be driving around the neighborhood. Flag us down and let us know if you see him." He turned toward the driver and they pulled away from the curb.

"I w-w-will," Jean said as she watched them leave. She went back to the children.

Later that day, as she was getting ready to leave, Jean told Mr. Morgan what the officer had asked her.

"And tomorrow they'll be looking for someone else," he said, barely glancing up from the papers he was signing at his desk. "That's how it goes."

The sun was beating down on them and the other groups had gone inside, but Jean's girls did not want to go in the building. They were having too much fun learning double Dutch jump rope moves. Jean had taught them how to run into the turning ropes two girls at a time and then, in unison, turn to the north, south, east, and west.

"I've almost got it!" one of the girls said.

"I told you it would be easy once you got the hang of it!" Jean said.

Then Jean heard the whoops. On the other side of the playground, standing against the wall of the recreation center, she saw a group of older teenage boys—maybe some in their early twenties—who had started what she could tell right away was a crap game. A young man in the middle of the group threw the dice against the wall, and when they bounced back into the dirt, they all stared down at the ground. Then there was laughter.

Someone shouted, "Beat that one, JD, beat that one!"

Another said, "Put some money down, why don't you. Or are you too broke?"

Laughter again.

Jean looked around for Mr. Morgan. He was not on the playfield. She said to the girls, "Stay right here and keep the ropes going, girls, I'll be right back."

Jean ran into the building and in a matter of seconds returned to the playground holding a megaphone. She held it close to her mouth and, mimicking what she had heard Mr. Morgan say as he broke up other craps games, yelled in the direction of the players, "Scatter!"

The game continued. More laughter.

"JD's out! Let me show you how to roll . . ."

Jean took a deep breath. She bellowed, "OK fellas, time to scatter!"

The young men looked over in Jean's direction.

"Aw, man, it's just a girl . . ."

"Naw, man, look, we gotta go. C'mon!"

Someone picked up the dice. They turned and ran off the playfield.

Jean turned to take the megaphone back inside the building when she saw Mr. Morgan standing in the doorway, looking at her and smiling. He walked toward her and took the megaphone.

"Good job," he said. He paused. "What are you studying at the university?"

"Science education," Jean answered.

"I've been watching you. You're good with the young ones. If you change your mind about teaching science, you're welcome to work for the recreation department full-time. I can get you an assignment, at a better place even. Just say the word."

"Thank you, Mr. Morgan, but I want to finish school and teach," Jean said.

"I'm just saying, if you change your mind."

Mr. Morgan started the Thursday evening square dances at six o'clock sharp. He was the caller. Jean and the other captains were there to act as chaperones. Mr. Morgan instructed newcomers in the basic moves. Then he divided the room into groups, four couples to a square. If there were extra couples after the squares were made, those couples rotated in and out of the dances throughout the evening. Everyone danced.

Mr. Morgan turned on the record player and started calling the moves. It was easy to hear his deep, bass voice calling over the music.

Honor your partner.
Honor your corner.
Swing your partner.
Swing your corner.
Now swing your partner once again.
And promenade around the ring. Promenade until you come back home.
Now face your partner . . . and a do-si-do . . .

Jean saw Mr. Morgan look at her and nod toward the girl's bathroom. That was the signal for Jean to make a bathroom check. She walked in and saw three teen girls; one was at the sink splashing water on her neck and down her blouse.

"I can't go home smelling like this," the girl at the sink was saying.

The other girls giggled.

"OK," Jean said. "You girls need to be on the dance floor. Let's go!"

"Aw, c'mon," the second girl said. "We gotta get cleaned up."

"You can clean up at home. Come join the square dance. You'll see, it's fun," Jean said.

"Who do you think you are?" the third girl asked.

"Shush," the girl at the sink said. "Leave it. We'll go."

Girl number two looked at Jean. "I've seen you before. Aren't you one of the Ford sisters . . . from over on Halleck Street?" she asked.

Jean was taken by surprise that this girl knew the family name and where she lived. "Yes. Yes, I am. Do you know my family?"

"No," the second girl answered. "Well, not really. But my mama knows Mrs. Rogers from over on Burnside. And Mrs. Rogers knows your mother."

"You're right, she does," Jean said.

"The other day I was over there at Mrs. Rogers's house with my mama," girl number two continued, "and we saw you walking down the street. Mrs. Rogers told my mama and me who you were."

"I was probably on my way to teach a piano lesson," Jean said.

Girl number two looked at her friend at the sink as she spoke. "She told my mama that all of the Ford girls are in college, that they're all good girls, pretty with nice hair . . ."

"Yeah, so what about it? You think that's something?" said the third girl.

"Well, I'm just sayin' what Mrs. Rogers said," the second girl replied.

"C'mon. Let's get outta here," said the girl at the sink. She brushed up against Jean muttering, "Stuck up college girl," as she left the bathroom.

The other two girls followed close behind her as they crossed the dance floor and left the building.

Jean waited a bit, then followed the girls out of the building to see if they were actually going home or hanging around outside the door. The girls were gone. She noticed a few men, young men in their twenties, standing off to the side, but didn't think anything of it. She looked more closely to see if they had liquor bottles in their hands, but their hands were empty. Jean was about to turn toward the door and go back inside when she felt something bump up against her from behind. A hand snaked across her mouth, and another hand gripped her upper arm, pushing her against the brick wall next to the door.

"Get over here, girl," a man demanded in a low, deep voice.

Oh no! What . . .

Jean tried to pull away.

This can't be happening to me!

The man squeezed her arm tighter. "Where do you think you're going?" he whispered, his mouth close to her ear.

Jean flashed back to that night on Belle Isle.

Me, walking alone along the dirt path. Too cheap to pay the dime it cost to get on the bus that would take me off the island. Then out of nowhere, Come here girl, a man snarled. He lunged out of the bushes toward me. I screamed and started to run. I barely saw his face or the color of his hands. I couldn't tell if he was white or just a light-skinned Negro. Get over here, he said. He reached out, running behind me. I tried to run faster. The ground turned muddy. I slipped and fell forward with my face, my purse, and the front of my blouse and skirt all in the mud. The sloppy wet dirt smelled like pee. The man reached down and grabbed my leg. Gotcha, he growled. But the mud must've made my skin slippery because my leg slipped right through his grip. Holding tight to my purse strap, I scrambled to get on all fours, then I pushed myself to my feet and started running again. Come back here, he slurred. I heard him spit and curse.

I ran until I reached the bus stop; no one else was there. I leaned forward, trying to catch my breath. I picked up some leaves I saw scattered on the ground and tried to wipe the mud off of my skirt, my blouse, but I just ended up rubbing the dirt in even deeper. And I smelled like pee.

The bus arrived. The bus driver stared at me as I mounted the steps. I fumbled along the bottom of my purse until I found the fare to put in the box. As I walked down the aisle to find a seat, I felt like all eyes were on me. I knew I looked like what Mama would call a hot mess, but I didn't care. I just wanted to find a seat and get home.

By the time I got off at the stop where I needed to transfer to the next bus, the mud had dried a bit and I was able to brush some of it off, but I couldn't brush off the pee smell. I knew I still looked a sight because folks on the bus stared at me. I found a seat and had almost dozed off when the driver announced, Next stop Dequindre! I got off the bus and hurried down Dequindre to Halleck Street. I hoped none of the neighbors saw me. I didn't want word to get out that I came home covered in mud. I turned up the driveway and walked up the steps to the back porch. The pee smell in my clothes seemed stronger now that I was back home. I closed the back door and walked into the kitchen. Mama let out a scream. Oh my baby, she yelled out. Goodness Lord, what happened to you? Before I could explain, Laura and Annie May came out of the bedroom, pushing each other out of the way to get through the door. Eeew! You smell, one of them said to me, I forget which one. The other one said, You're covered in mud! I heard Daddy's heavy footsteps as he strode into the kitchen. Then his voice, Good God, child, you tell me what happened, and you tell me right now! he demanded.

I told them all about taking the path through the woods and the man who jumped out of nowhere.

Daddy interrupted me, Did he touch you?

I could hear the anger in Daddy's voice.

No Daddy, I explained, I fell in the mud and he grabbed my foot, but I got away.

Did he touch you again? I shook my head, no. Did he do anything else to you? Daddy asked. I could see the anger in his face: his eyebrows were furrowed tight, his lips were squeezed together. I had never seen him look like that before.

No, Daddy, no, I said, looking straight at him. He didn't touch me again. He didn't do anything else. I ran away before—

"What's going on out here?" It was Mr. Morgan.

The man had Jean pressed up against the brick wall. His hand still covered her mouth. His body was pushed up against hers.

Mr. Morgan grabbed the man's arms and yanked him off Jean. Mr. Morgan was taller than the other man and twice as wide.

"Miss Ford, get back inside," he said, teeth clenched.

Jean pulled away and stood at the door, her arms folded across her chest, her body shaking.

"You scumbag, you low-life piece of swine! How dare you come around here and lay hands on one of my staff!"

Jean watched as Mr. Morgan grabbed the man by his collar and pulled him up close. The man's head was tilted back as he looked up at Mr. Morgan.

"I'm going to say this one time and one time only—if you so much as look like you're going to touch one of my staff, I'm not gonna call the police." Mr. Morgan jerked the man up, pulling him up off the ground. But the man's head was still bent back. It looked like Mr. Morgan was talking to his chin.

"No sir, I'll tell you what I'll do—" Mr. Morgan took a step forward and pushed the man hard up against the brick wall. "I'll tell you what I'll do—I'll kill you myself!" he said. He let the man drop to the ground. "Now, get outta here!" Mr. Morgan roared.

The man ran off.

"The rest of you thugs, go on now! And don't come back around here!" he hollered to the rest of the men who were standing around, watching.

Mr. Morgan turned and walked over to Jean. He put his hands on her shoulders and guided her body toward the door. "Let's go inside, now," he said. Then he lowered his hands and let her enter the building first.

The music was still playing, but the dancing had stopped. Jean could see that all eyes were on them as she and Mr. Morgan entered the room. She tried to stand erect, as if nothing was wrong, but even then, she knew her hair was mussed. Jean could tell: everyone there knew something had happened.

They probably heard Mr. Morgan. Mr. Morgan's voice got loud toward the end. Oh, Lord, there'll be gossip for sure!

"Davis?" Mr. Morgan said, pointing to one of the other captains. "Get the dancing started again. You do the calls. I'll be back shortly," Mr. Morgan said, then walked toward his office; Jean followed close behind.

"Rest here awhile," he said as he closed the door and led her to one of the chairs in front of his desk. "Let me get you a drink of water."

"No, I'm fine, Mr. Morgan, really I am," Jean said, trying to steady her voice. She was shaking inside. She could still taste the dirt from the man's hand against her mouth. She could still feel his breath as he talked into her ear.

He called me college girl. College girl won't be a good girl for long, he said to me . . . I got you, college girl.

"I'm going to call your father and have him pick you up," Mr. Morgan said.

Jean sat up straight, shaking the memory of that man from her thoughts as she shook her head.

"No, no, please don't do that," she said. "Don't call my daddy. He won't let me work here again if he knew what happened," Jean pleaded.

Mr. Morgan sighed. "Well, all right. But I'll stand with you at the bus stop until you get on the bus."

"Thank you," she said. Then she added in a low voice, "I'd like to go now, if that's all right with you."

"Of course."

"Just let me go to the rest room," Jean said, as she got up and turned toward Mr. Morgan's office door. "I need to wash my face before I go home."

12

1950

NURSERY RHYMES

"Wake up, Jean!"

Jean sat up, startled, as she opened her eyes. It was Carlton. His hand was gently shaking her arm and her hand was empty; her sandwich had fallen onto her lap.

"Oh, goodness," Jean said. Then she looked around the cafeteria in the basement of Old Main to see if anyone else had noticed that she had dozed off while eating her lunch. Old Main was what everyone called the majestic, massive-looking building located smack dab in the middle of campus where almost all the classes offered by the university were held. Romanesque Revival was the style of architecture, or at least that's what the dedication plaque bolted above the cornerstone said.

Jean looked around again: no one seemed to notice that her sandwich had come apart in her lap. She put the slice of ham back between the two slices of bread.

"You're going to choke to death if you don't watch out," Carlton said.

"I'll be fine," Jean said. "Really. It's just that it's been quite a week. My piano students—I've given two lessons already this week. Thank goodness one student canceled. I worked the square dance last night at Cardoni. Then I was up late last night finishing my semester project for my Elementary Early Grades Methods course. I'm going to turn it in to Professor Caldwell after my next class."

Ever since receiving the assignment from Professor Louise Caldwell early in the winter semester of her junior year, Jean had put in long hours on the project. She decided to make practical use of her classical training on the piano—those many years of weekly music lessons for her and her sisters, each girl taking their turn at the grand piano in Mrs. Lewis's living room—to create melodies and harmonies for some of the most popular nursery rhymes. Rhymes like "Baa Baa Black Sheep," "Hickory Dickory Dock," "Humpty Dumpty," "Jack and Jill," and "Mary Had a Little Lamb"—Jean took those and several more, for a total of fifteen, and composed melody lines with accompanying chord progressions that were original and unique for each one. From the talk among the students both before and after class, and without sharing her own details, she didn't think anyone else in the class had chosen a project like hers. Jean was sure she'd get an A grade from Professor Caldwell, who had a reputation among the education students for being a hard grader, both on the project and in the class.

"Want me to buy you a cup of coffee?" Carlton asked, gently nudging her arm. "Help you stay awake?"

"No, thanks, really," Jean said. "I'll be fine. I just want to finish this sandwich before class."

While she was eating, Carlton greeted a friend who was walking by. The friend stopped and Carlton introduced Jean to Vincent Bellamy. Jean was chewing a mouthful of ham and bread, so she just smiled and nodded.

Jean didn't really consider Carlton Montgomery her boyfriend. They had been spending time together, on and off, for just over a year. He would take her to a movie downtown maybe once a month. There were not many social activities where Negro students were welcome on Wayne University's campus. Even certain restaurants near campus made it clear that Negro students were not wanted as customers. Negro fraternities and sororities filled the void. Like most of the Negro students, Jean had pledged a sorority—she had waited until her sophomore year—and Carlton had pledged a fraternity. If she saw him at one of their socials, he would ask her to dance and maybe take her out for ice cream afterwards.

"I like Carlton and all," she would explain to her friends when they whispered about who was a couple and who wasn't. "He's nice and he's fun to be with, but I have my classes to finish, and I don't want anything to get in the way of me getting my teaching degree on time. I'm just not ready for a serious boyfriend."

While they never talked about it directly, Jean got the feeling that Carlton was fine keeping their relationship just as it was.

At first, Jean and the others cast sideways glances at one another—then they got used to her presence—when Carrie Sue often sat with them in the small cafeteria located in the basement of Old Main and ate her lunch at one of the tables with the other Negro students. She listened intently as they discussed their perspective on some of the issues that were important to them: postwar economic opportunities; the effect of the newly integrated armed forces on the rest of American society; social integration; and their responsibilities as part of Detroit's burgeoning Negro middle class. But the whispers really started when some of them saw her dancing with her boyfriend at the jukebox the university installed in the cafeteria late in Jean's junior year.

"Lord have mercy, look at that girl move! She has some Negro blood in her, for sure!" Jean heard some of her friends say, chuckling, as they watched.

"I've seen other white folks who can dance," one said.

"Yeah, but she puts a little something extra in those moves. No, somewhere down the line some Negro blood snuck into her family tree," another replied. Others watching from across the room laughed and murmured in agreement.

So, when Carrie Sue leaned in close to Jean as they both sat eating their sandwiches, lowering her voice so much that Jean could barely hear her, and said, "I'm an octoroon," Jean wasn't all that surprised. Carrie Sue wasn't telling her anything she or any of the other Negro students hadn't already suspected. And just as Jean was working backwards in her head, trying to figure out exactly how many generations ago that miscegenation took place in order to make this white girl one-eighth Negro, Carrie Sue said, "My great-granddaddy was a Negro."

According to Carrie Sue, "Great-grandma told her daddy she was gonna have a baby and the father was a Negro man she'd been sneaking out with at night over at the loading docks. She'd met him one evening when she was coming out of the fish market. He was delivering a load of fish from his ship. He was a free Negro, one of the seamen that went from port to port up and down the Atlantic coast. Her daddy was furious. Said he was gonna get the Klan on that Negro, free man or not. But my great-grandma begged him not to. Said how she loved him, and he might as well get the Klan on her, too. So he said once she'd birthed it he'd take the mongrel and drown it in the creek behind their house."

Jean listened to the story and nodded as Carrie Sue kept talking. Jean wanted to finish eating and hurry up to the third floor because she thought there was a good chance grades for the semester projects were posted by now.

Why—out of all the Negroes on campus—did Carrie Sue decide to confide in me? And today of all days! I really just want to get upstairs and find out my project grade.

"But when the baby was born, it came out so light-skinned that my great-grandma's daddy changed his mind saying that the child looked white and he couldn't bring himself to kill a white baby. He got a second cousin to marry my great-grandma and when anyone said anything about the child's swarthy color—especially in the summer months, what with playing in the hot sun and all—they just said it was from their Indian blood from way back." Carrie Sue shook her head. "Indian blood covered up a multitude of sins back in the day," she said to Jean.

Jean stopped nodding as soon as she realized Carrie Sue had finished her story. "You're right about that Indian blood, Carrie Sue," Jean said. "More than any of us will probably ever know."

"And you won't tell anyone, will you?" Carrie Sue asked, her voice still a whisper. "About my great-granddaddy and all?"

"Oh, never, Carrie Sue," Jean answered. "Your secret's good with me. I won't tell a soul."

𝕸

Jean stepped back from the paper posted to the wall. She was stunned.

That can't be right!

She stepped forward and looked at the paper again, closer this time. She found her name and looked across to the grade column.

Grade–F. An F. An F? That's gotta be some kind of mistake. All the time I put into this, all those melodies and chords . . .

Jean rushed down the hall and stopped in front of Professor Caldwell's door.

She'd better be in her office!

Jean scanned the papers tacked to the door for some mention of office hours, all the while knocking on the door, when the voice from inside the room said, "Come in!"

Jean entered quickly. Professor Caldwell looked up from her seat behind her desk, a cup of coffee in her hand.

"Professor Caldwell—I'm Jean Ford."

"Yes, I know. How can I help you?"

"My grade—you posted an F. There must be some mistake."

"No mistake, Miss Ford. Your grade is an F because I never received your project."

"What? I put the envelope in your mailbox. Before the due date, even! You must have seen it. I wrote music, original music, to accompany fifteen nursery rhymes."

The woman held up her hand. Jean went silent.

"Miss Ford, I never received your project."

"Well, I kept a draft copy of the songs at home. I can write out another for you tonight. I can put it in your hands tomorrow."

Professor Caldwell stood up. "It will still be late. Your grade won't change."

"But what will that do to my semester grade?"

"That's not my concern. I never received the project. The F stands."

Jean started breathing quickly. She felt light-headed, almost faint.

"Good day, Miss Ford."

Jean wasn't sure if she said goodbye to the woman or not. She turned quickly and left the room, closing the door behind her.

This can't be happening to me. I know I turned the project in. I put the envelope in her mailbox. There were other envelopes there too. I saw them.

Still feeling faint, Jean made her way down the hallway, touching her hand against the wall to steady herself as she walked. She found herself at the staircase. She sat down at the top of the stairs and leaned forward with her head almost in her lap.

An F? How? And she won't let me turn in another copy? What happened to my project?

"Jean?"

Jean looked up. Carrie Sue was standing on the top step next to her.

"Jean, you don't look so good. Are you all right?"

Jean shook her head. Then she said, "No. Something terrible just happened."

"Well come up off the stairs. Someone's going to trip over you or you're going to fall . . . either way you need to move."

Carrie Sue helped Jean stand up.

"I was just studying in an empty classroom down the hall. We can go back in there and talk."

Jean followed her down the hall and into the classroom. Carrie Sue closed the door behind them.

"So what happened?" Carrie Sue asked as she led Jean to an empty desk and sat down beside her.

Jean took a deep breath and slowly exhaled. Then she proceeded to tell Carrie Sue about the nursery rhymes and how she had written original melodies and chord progressions and even turned the project in before the due date.

"I put so much work into that project, I just knew I had gotten an A!" Jean said. Then she paused.

"When I went to see the posted grades, I had an F."

Carrie Sue gasped.

"Yes, she gave me an F! I ran to Professor Caldwell's office. She says she never got the envelope I put in her mailbox. She said she gave me an F because she never received the project. Can you believe that? She says she never got it. And I can't bring in the copy I have at home because she says the project is late now, and she said I would still get an F because it's late."

By then, Carrie Sue's jaw had dropped.

"Jean, you aren't going to believe this, but I know what happened to your project," she said in a low voice.

"What? That's impossible! How do you know?" Jean asked.

Even though she was sitting at a desk, Carrie Sue put her hand on her hip as if she were standing. "I know what happened because I was in the Education Department offices just yesterday talking to a secretary, trying to make an appointment with one of my professors. There were two women talking in a corner. Talking in low voices, but I could still make out what they were saying. From what you just told me, now I know that one of them was your Professor Caldwell."

"How do you know that?" Jean asked.

"By what she was saying to the other woman. Don't you see? People say things around me because they think I'm one of them. Because I look like them. But they don't know . . . they don't know what you know about me."

"What were they saying, Carrie Sue? Tell me!" Jean reached over and grabbed her by the wrist.

"I heard her say—your Professor Caldwell—I heard her say she didn't want any of your classmates to think that a darkie was capable of doing a project like that. That in all her years teaching at the university, she'd never had a student do a project like that—put her own music to a whole set of nursery rhymes!"

"What? Oh, dear Lord!" Jean let go of Carrie Sue's wrist. She put her hands up to her face and shook her head hard. "How could she say that? How could she do this to me?"

Carrie Sue raised her voice. "Professor Caldwell said, 'No, I'm putting a stop to it right now. She gets an F!' And then the other woman started talking about one of her students, and then both of them walked out of the office. I don't think either of them ever noticed I was standing right there. Or maybe they didn't care."

That evening at home, Jean sat at the kitchen table and watched as her mother stirred a pot of chicken and dumplings over at the stove. May Ford was back to cooking like she used to before Laura started at the University of Michigan—making meals in the middle of the week that took a long time at the stove, like chicken and dumplings or pot roast and biscuits. She said she had time now because Laura was about to graduate that June. Jean had watched as her mother wrote that final check to the University of Michigan for Laura's room and board, and, as she was writing, said she was going to quit doing day work as soon as she mailed the check. And that's what she had done: May Ford announced at dinner the day she mailed that check that she had given Mrs. Patterson one week's notice. She was done.

"Mama?" Jean asked, still watching her.

"Yes, baby," her mother answered.

"You remember the music I wrote to all those nursery rhymes for that special project? For my methods class?" Jean asked her.

"Oh course, how could I forget watching you hunched over the piano, listening to you late at night working on those songs. Yes, I remember!"

"Well this afternoon after lunch I went to see if my grade was posted and . . ." Jean proceeded to tell her mother about seeing an F grade posted on the wall and what Professor Caldwell said when Jean went to her office.

"Oh no, baby! Oh, Jean, good Lord!" May said, over and over, shaking her head.

But when Jean told her mother about how Carrie Sue found her sitting at the top of the steps, she had to backtrack and explain about Carrie Sue's great-granddaddy being a Negro.

"Shush! She told you that?" May Ford said.

"Yes, Mama, she whispered that she was an octoroon. She told me everything."

"So she and that whole bloodline, they're passing," May said.

"I hadn't thought about it like that," Jean said, "but I guess you're right. They have been."

"Happens more than you'd know, child, more than you'd know."

"Well because everyone thinks she's white . . ." And then Jean proceeded to tell her mother what Carrie Sue had heard Professor Caldwell say to the other professor in the College of Education offices.

By that time, May had walked over to where Jean sat at the kitchen table. Jean felt her mother's hands as she put one on Jean's shoulder and began stroking her hair with the other.

"This is a hard pill for you to swallow, I know it is," her mother said. Then she pulled a chair closer to Jean and sat down. "But at least you found out why you got that failing grade. You know, up front, that race had everything to do with it."

Jean felt tears welling up in her eyes. Her nose started running and she wiped the wetness with her sleeve. Then she reached for the handkerchief her mother had just pulled from her apron pocket and blew her nose into it.

Mama's going to keep talking, trying to make me feel better. But should I feel better knowing that the grade is not just about me, Jean Ford? That the professor gave me an F on my project because she doesn't want anyone to know that a Negro—any Negro—is good enough and smart enough to put music to nursery rhymes? Uh-uh, it was my grade. No matter what Professor Caldwell feels about every other Negro that walks on this earth—it was my grade! She gave me, Jean Ford, an F. No, I don't feel better!

Jean blew her nose again.

The Negro burden. That's what Mama always calls it.

May Ford was still talking. Jean listened. "Especially your father and I coming from the South, where race is everything. Everything, child. And up North, when I came up here with your father, I found out quickly enough that it can be the same way here. Look at how the Teamsters wouldn't let your father become a member because they didn't allow Negroes in their union, and him with a fleet of trucks for his wood business for goodness' sake. Or your father having to use the driver Jim Hines in his business just so he and his other drivers could go through the gates of those auto factories to get to their old wooden crates. No, whether you live in the North or in the South, this is America. This is how it is for Negroes in America; the burden that's put on us."

The Negro burden. I hear you, Mama.

Jean wiped her eyes with the handkerchief.

But an F—she gave me an F, after all that work I did, just because I'm a Negro and because she doesn't want anyone to think that a Negro is capable of doing a project like the one I gave her.

"There's no way around it," her mother said, standing up at the table. "We tried to raise you so that you would be strong enough to shake off that burden. And I think we've done that. You children have overcome and excelled at every turn. And I'm so proud of my babies."

I hear you, Mama.

May bent over and kissed Jean on the forehead.

"Thank you, Mama," Jean said.

Jean watched as her mother went back to the stove and stirred the chicken and dumplings.

"You'll feel better after you've eaten a good meal," her mother said as she worked at the stove.

No, Mama. No, I won't. Because I still got an F on that project I worked so hard on. I still got an F because I'm a Negro.

13

1951

WEDDING DRESS

Jean Ford stood in front of the full-length mirror in the fitting room of the Kelly Bridal Shop. Her lips were quivering as she fought back the tears.

"I can't get married in this dress—this dress is hideous! I won't wear it!" Jean blurted out, tears streaming down her cheeks.

"Now dear," May Ford said. "Patsy paid one hundred twenty-five dollars for this dress—you'll never get a better one. This is the one you'll wear."

Jean's mouth fell open. "But Mama . . ."

"It's a fine dress. You won't do any better."

"But Mama, it's Patsy's dress!"

"She looked beautiful in it and so will you."

"But look at it," Jean said, turning from one side to the other in front of the mirror. "The dress hangs on me like a sack! How can I wear this gown?" Jean asked, crying even harder.

"Calm down, child," her mother said. "The owner will know how to alter it so that it fits you perfectly. I promise."

"And the headpiece, it's hideous! It looks like someone stuck a fan on the tip of my head!"

"No, dear, it's a mantilla. And with your hair brushed back in an upsweep, you'll look lovely wearing that headpiece. You'll be a beautiful bride, you'll see," May said.

"Oh, Mama, no!"

"Here," May said. She took a handkerchief from her purse and handed it to Jean, who used it to wipe her eyes and blow her nose.

Once Jean had calmed down, as if on cue, the owner entered the dressing room. She was enthusiastic.

"Of course I remember making this gown for your sister. Beautiful! Wonderful for sisters to share a dress. Such special memories."

As she marked with pins and tailor's chalk where she would take in the seams, she chattered, "My dear, you are such a waif. So thin you are. I'll have to take this gown in—let's see here—three and one-half inches on each side. But you have more sisters? I'll save the extra fabric in a way so that your other sisters will be able to wear the dress if they need to take out the seams. Most dressmakers could not do that, but I am trained in the old school. It can be done. Yes, all sisters sharing the dress . . . Won't that be a wonderful thing!"

When Jean and her mother got back home, Jean walked right into the bedroom without a word to Annie May, even though she saw her sister sitting at the kitchen table with a plate of something in front of her. She heard Annie May asking their mother, "What's wrong with her?"

Jean didn't wait for her mother's answer. She just pulled off her coat and sat down on the edge of the bed and shook her head.

Even if that woman takes in seams so that it fits like a glove, it's just an ugly dress. And that hideous headpiece . . . What am I going to do? What can I do? Mama says I'm going to wear it . . . Good Lord, who would've thought it—I'm in my senior year, Christmas is coming up, and I'm engaged to Vincent Bellamy. A year ago I didn't even know him. Today I got fitted for my wedding dress.

Jean lay back on the bed and closed her eyes, picturing how it all had happened and how much her life had changed in a very short time.

It had been close to the end of her junior year at Wayne University— shortly after her project received a failing grade from Professor Caldwell—when Vincent Bellamy started courting Jean Ford. It seemed to Jean that Carlton slowly faded out of her life and Vincent took his place. Until Carlton introduced the two of them that afternoon in the Old Main cafeteria, Jean had never noticed Vincent on campus before. After that first meeting, it seemed that Jean started bumping into him everywhere—on the way to class, in the library, even at a couple of the dances put on by his fraternity. At those parties, he always asked her to dance, and later in the evening, they would sit down together and chat for a while. Then, after getting to know him at those dances, instead of Carlton it was Vincent who would meet her in the Old Main cafeteria so that they could eat their lunch together. It was after finishing his sandwich one day that Vincent asked her out on their first date.

"My fraternity's having a convocation for the graduates," he said after clearing his throat. "It's this Saturday. Would you like to go with me?"

"Sure," Jean answered. "Yes I would." She gave him her address—1950 Halleck Street, near Davison.

"I'll find it," he said. "I'll pick you up on Saturday at six o'clock."

At six o'clock exactly, Vincent arrived at the Ford front door. Jean greeted him and introduced him to her parents. Douglas Ford got up from his chair in the living room, pipe still clenched between his teeth, and extended his hand. While Vincent shook his hand, May Ford emerged from the kitchen.

"Good evening, Mr. and Mrs. Ford," Vincent said.

"Glad to meet you, young man," Jean's father said.

"Please, have a seat," Jean's mother said, motioning toward the sofa.

Jean sat next to him. But noticing her mother's eyes upon her, did not sit too close.

"So, what do you do, young man?" her father asked bluntly.

Vincent cleared his throat. "Sir, right now, I work part-time at the university library. But I'll graduate at the end of this semester with a degree in education. I've already enrolled in the graduate school's program in educational administration." He paused. Douglas Ford puffed on his pipe as he listened.

"And, I've been hired by the Detroit Public Schools as a special education teacher at Jacoby School."

Jean looked at Vincent in surprise. "You didn't tell me," she said.

"I was going to tell you this evening. I just got the letter today," Vincent said.

"Jacoby School's near Cardoni," Jean said, looking first at her father and then her mother.

Jean's father emptied the bowl of his pipe into an ashtray. "Jean tells me you're a veteran," her father said.

"Yes, sir," Vincent said.

"Our son served in the Army, in Italy," her father continued.

"I served in the Army, sir. I was an NCO, master sergeant, in India," Vincent said. "Kanchrapara, India, sir, near Calcutta."

Her father stood up. "So where are you taking my daughter this evening?" he asked.

Vincent stood up as well. He described his fraternity's convocation service at a church on Woodward Avenue.

"How will you get there?"

"On the bus, sir."

"Well, then, be on your way," he said, holding his hand out. He and Vincent shook hands.

"Have her home before midnight."

"Yes, sir."

OOO

Jean leaned forward on the bed, resting on her elbow. She could hear Annie in the kitchen, still chattering away to their mother.

I want to talk to Mama, too! Whatever they have to talk about can wait!

Then Jean lay back down, unable to shake the memories of how she became engaged to Vincent Bellamy.

OOO

"OK, I'll be ready at five," Jean said and hung up the phone. It was midsummer, before the start of her senior year, and one of the sororities was hosting a barbecue at a park near campus. Vincent had phoned to tell her that he would pick up a fraternity brother and his date, then swing around and pick her up. Vincent had bought a car by then, and he often planned double dates with his friends, usually to a movie theater downtown or—crossing the Ambassador Bridge over the Detroit River and into Canada—a day at the beach. He liked the beach at Point Pelee on Lake Erie. Jean liked that they could see each other without having to worry about bus routes and schedules, especially on weekends.

What little free time she had, what with working at Cardoni and giving piano lessons, Jean spent with Vincent. And between his teaching summer school at Jacoby and taking graduate school courses, she knew it was the same for him. Before long, Jean and Vincent were known around campus as a couple. With as much time as they spent together, Jean herself felt like they were a couple.

Jean liked to recall the time Vincent surprised her—they were at the beach at Point Pelee, with two other couples. It was getting close to evening, and Jean and Vincent were sitting on a large boulder close to the water. The tide was coming in over their feet. It was chilly, and Vincent had put his jacket over Jean's shoulders. Then he turned to her and took her hand in his. "It was love at first sight, for me. I've loved you since I first laid eyes on you, sitting there eating a sandwich in the cafeteria."

Jean gasped. She didn't know what to say. Other than Carlton, she had never really dated. And she didn't know what being in love should feel like. She liked Vincent, that much she knew. She liked him a lot. She enjoyed being with him and being known as a couple around campus.

Maybe this is what love feels like: I like being around him. He's just nice to be around.

Jean stuttered something, but no real words came out.

"You don't have to say a thing," he said. "I just wanted you to know." Then, he put his arm around her and pulled her closer to him.

At home, her parents let her know that they approved of him. Her father came straight to the point. "I like that young man," he said to her one evening, out of the blue, looking at her over his newspaper. "He looks you straight in the eye. He has a firm grip when he shakes your hand. He's going to be somebody," he told her. "Mark my words." And then he went back to reading his newspaper.

Her mother didn't say much one way or the other, but that told Jean all that she needed to know. If her mother didn't voice disapproval, then that meant she liked Vincent.

m

Vincent never directly asked Jean to marry him. It was after Thanksgiving Day, and Jean was back in school. Vincent picked her up after her last class, at the end of his workday. After telling Jean they were going shopping, Vincent took her to a jeweler on Washington Boulevard. Once inside, he pointed out two rings beneath a glass counter.

"Pick one," he said.

"What's this for?" Jean asked.

"To get married!" Vincent announced.

Jean was stunned. Her eyesight blurred. Both engagement rings looked the same to her mind's haze: diamonds on a band of white gold. She nervously picked the ring on the left that had a larger diamond in the center with smaller diamonds on the band on either side of it.

"I thought you might pick that one," Vincent said. "Wait right here."

Vincent walked over to a salesclerk and pointed and whispered. All sorts of thoughts were running through her head.

Married? Me, married? So this is how it happens. This is how you get married? Funny, I've never thought about getting married. Even when Patsy was engaged and planning her wedding, I never thought it might be me one day. I've just thought about how I would finish school and teach somewhere in Detroit. They don't have boardinghouses in Detroit, not that I know of. Not like in the South when Mama was a teacher in Clarksville. And Mama and Daddy would never let me live in one of those apartment buildings for single women—no, never! No, I pictured myself living at home and teaching.

The clerk came over to Jean and measured her finger for the ring size.

"Best wishes," the clerk said as he wrote down the size number. "You've selected a lovely ring."

Jean nodded and smiled in response.

So this is how it goes . . .

Jean had seen the groups of giggling girls gathering around a friend who'd just gotten her engagement ring. Sometimes, especially if it was one of her sorority sisters, she'd be one of the crowd, giggling and oohing at the size of the diamond.

Now I'll be the one holding up my hand, my ring finger in full view . . . And I can still teach. Nothing says I can't be married and still be a teacher. My friends at school, my sorority sisters—they all plan to teach, get married, have a family. Patsy has a baby boy now, and she swears she's going back to her classroom. Mama says she'll look after the boy during the day. She'll do the same for me, I know she will.

"In one week," the clerk said to Vincent.

The only difference I can think of right now . . . instead of calling me Miss Ford, the children in my classroom will call me Mrs. Bellamy.

During that next week, Jean didn't speak to anyone about the ring: not her sorority sisters, not her sisters at home, not her parents. No one except Vincent. As they sat huddled together in the cafeteria at Old Main, the two of them discussed wedding dates and selected a date next spring on his birthday, March 24, 1951. Another day, they talked about where they might live. Vincent had been looking at houses on Detroit's northwest side, an area quickly filling with the Negro middle class as whites moved out to the suburbs or died off. He drove Jean by a brick bungalow that he thought they could afford, if it stayed on the market. Jean was smitten with the house, and that same night, she started looking at newspaper ads for furniture and carpeting.

Later in the week, when they were walking around downtown, looking at the Christmas decorations in the store windows, Vincent brought up the honeymoon. Jean shook her head.

"I'm just getting used to the idea of getting married," she said. "I can't even think about a honeymoon! You pick wherever you think would be a nice place."

"Well, I'd rather put my money toward the house instead of an expensive honeymoon," he said. "Let's just go someplace nice nearby."

They settled on a weekend in Canada, about a one-hour drive

away once they crossed the bridge, in the small tourist town of Amherstburg.

One week from the day that he purchased the ring, Vincent phoned Jean and asked if he could come by and speak to her father. She told him that her father was out seeing about one of the trucks he'd leased to the city. He'd be home later that night. Vincent was insistent, so Jean invited him over to play cards and wait.

Annie May and Laura were home, so the four of them sat at the kitchen table and played a few hands of bridge. As the evening wore on, Annie May excused herself and got ready for bed. Jean, Laura, and Vincent played a couple of hands of three-handed bridge. But when Laura left for bed as well, Jean said, "Enough cards. It's after eleven o'clock. I don't think you'll be seeing my father tonight."

"I'd like to stay a little longer, if it's all right with you and your mother."

"Mama?" Jean asked, raising her voice a bit.

May Ford had been sitting in the living room throughout the evening, reading magazines and listening to the radio. But Jean knew her mother would have also been listening to every word being said in the kitchen.

"Vincent, dear, Jean's curfew is midnight. You can wait until then," May said.

Jean and Vincent joined her mother in the living room. While they listened to the radio, Jean felt herself dozing off. Then the front door opened.

Vincent stood as Douglas Ford entered the living room. Jean saw the look of surprise on her father's face.

"Why are you still here, young man—almost past Jean's curfew?" Douglas asked.

"I've been waiting to talk to you, sir," Vincent answered. Then he turned to Jean and asked, "Jean, can you please excuse yourself to another room?"

May stayed seated but put her magazine down on the coffee table. Jean went into the kitchen. From where she sat at the table, she could see and hear Vincent and her father in the living room.

"Mr. Ford," Vincent said, the two of them still standing, "I would like permission to marry your daughter."

"Let's sit down," Douglas said, gesturing toward the two chairs by the radio cabinet. "Do you have a date in mind?" Douglas asked, settling in his seat.

"Yes, sir—next year—March 24," Vincent answered.

"Do you promise to take care of her?"

"Yes, sir."

"Will you make sure she finishes school after the wedding and graduates next June?"

"Yes, sir."

"All right then, young man, you have my permission."

"Thank you, sir!" Vincent stood with his arm outstretched. Jean's father stood as well. They shook hands. Vincent walked over to Jean's mother, still seated, and shook her hand.

Vincent went to the kitchen and knelt next to where Jean sat. Jean felt tears welling up in her eyes. He put the ring on her finger, kissed her hand, then kissed her lips.

"I love you, Jean," Vincent said in a low voice. "I've told you before—it was love at first sight, from the first moment we met. And I'll be proud to have you as my wife."

Tears streamed down her cheeks. "I'll be proud to be your wife, Vincent," Jean said, her voice quivering. Then she said, for the first time to herself and to him, almost inaudibly, "I love you, too."

Jean saw Vincent look up at the kitchen clock. It was midnight, and they both knew he would have to leave.

And now she was stuck with that hideous dress. Out of nowhere,

Jean felt a rush of heat course through her entire body. She sat up straight on the side of the bed. She started breathing quickly. The room began to spin around her.

What's happening to me? Why am I feeling this way? Am I going to faint? Am I going to die?

Her head throbbed. She couldn't catch her breath.

"Mama!" Jean screamed. "Mama!"

A pot crashed to the floor as May Ford rushed into the bedroom from the kitchen.

"Good Lord, what is it child!" May said.

"Mother, something's wrong with me! Help me!" Jean was still breathing quickly.

"What's wrong? What are you feeling—tell me!"

May walked over and put the back of her hand on Jean's forehead.

"I've just been lying here thinking about how I met Vincent and how he courted me and how we picked out the ring and he asked Daddy for permission to marry me . . . and then I felt hot all over. I thought I was going to faint, maybe even die! And now, now I'm thinking, well maybe I'm feeling this way because it's a sign . . ."

"A sign? What do you mean, child?" her mother asked, looking down at Jean.

"Maybe it's a sign that I shouldn't marry Vincent. That this is all a mistake!"

Jean watched as her mother reached over and pushed the bedroom door shut. Then she sat beside her on the bed.

"You know, it's perfectly normal to feel nervous before you get married."

"Mama, all I've ever wanted was to be a teacher, like you were. Why do I have to get married?"

"Oh, my dear child, you do not have to marry Vincent. No one's making you marry him. It's your choice and yours alone. But Vincent is a fine young man. He's treating you right, isn't he?"

"Yes, Mama, always. But I want to teach and have a classroom and then come home and live right here with you and Daddy," Jean said. "You lived on your own in a boardinghouse while you were a teacher and before you married Daddy. I want what you had!"

Jean felt her mother pull away. She watched as she straightened her back.

"Oh my dear daughter," May said. "Yes, I had a classroom and I lived in a boardinghouse. But it's not how you think. I was lonely. And I was miserable."

"What?" Jean looked at her mother, stunned.

Mama never talked like this before. When we were growing up, she always told us how happy she was as a teacher, how the owner of the boardinghouse took such good care of her. How she was treated with respect and honor.

"You never said—"

"I was an outcast because of my color, my education. The young men were afraid to court me, probably afraid of the whispers."

"What whispers?" Jean asked.

"Oh, people talk. My how they talk!" May said. "From the time that I was a little girl sitting on the front porch doing my needlework, folks would walk by, mostly women folk, and say just loud enough for me to hear, 'Raising those girls to think they're too good for the tobacco patch . . . just because they're high yellow and got good hair.' Oh yes people talk. 'She might look white, just because her daddy's white . . .' No, not many men could stand up to talk like that."

Her daddy's white. She just said it. I heard her. She said her daddy's white!

Before Jean knew it, before she could stop herself, she blurted out, "Mama, your daddy—he was white?"

There was silence between them.

"Yes," May said, "yes, he was."

"Who was he? Did you know him?"

"Yes, I knew him. At least, I knew who he was. He was the judge," her mother said flatly.

The judge? Good God, the judge!

Jean asked, "The judge you talked about so many times when we were all growing up? The one who bought you your books and—"

"The one who sent the colored woman who worked across town over to teach me needlework when I couldn't go to school after the fire. And, yes, he bought my schoolbooks and supplies every year. Had them delivered to the house, wrapped in brown paper. And he paid my way through Tennessee A&I. Even made provisions with the university for my tuition and room and board to be paid in the event of his death. Yes, he was the one Grandma Jackson worked for. She was his housekeeper. And Mr. Jackson worked as his porter after that. Yes, child, yes child."

Seems like all my life I heard about that judge. And now I know why. Oh my dear Lord . . . now I know why.

Jean took a deep breath.

"Mama," Jean said, haltingly. "How . . . why?"

"It's so hard to explain . . . so hard to explain. It was a different world back then. My mother—Grandma Jackson—she didn't have a choice. She couldn't help the hand she was dealt. No colored woman had a choice back then." May Ford stopped and looked straight ahead. Then she turned and looked at Jean.

"You have choices. Your father and I saw to it that you girls would have choices. And it's your choice now. So you decide, you and only you decide if you want to marry Vincent. He's a fine young man. He's got one degree, and he'll soon have another. You'll have a good future with him, with a home and family. I can feel it in my bones. And, if you decide you don't want to marry him, that's fine, too. But, please, whatever you do decide, *please* don't do it because you want to be like me."

May Ford leaned over and kissed Jean on the forehead. Then

Jean watched as her mother turned and left the room. She lay back down on the bed, flat on her back. Jean felt the tears welling up in her eyes. She turned away from the door, over on her side, pulling her knees up close to her chest. Then she quietly sobbed.

Mama never talked like that before, about being so miserable living on her own at that boardinghouse. We never heard that part of the story. And she'd shared so many stories with us girls about growing up in Clarksville, attending Tennessee A&I and living in the dormitory with Maddie and Hazel and her other friends, about being invited to be the new teacher at the colored school in Clarksville. About being treated with respect and high honor everywhere she went because she was a teacher. She never, not once, talked about being lonely, being miserable . . .

Jean put the palms of her hands up to her eyes and wiped away the tears.

So this is how it goes.

She shook her head. Then she stood up, stepped over to the dresser, and looked at herself in the mirror.

It all comes to this: I decide whether I put that wedding dress on or not . . . whether I marry Vincent, or not. It's my choice, mine alone.

EPILOGUE

The four Ford sisters all earned their bachelors and masters degrees and were educators in the Detroit Public schools: Maber Ford Hill retired as an elementary school reading specialist; Marion Ford Thomas retired as a high school science/mathematics department head; Jean Ford Fuqua retired as an elementary school teacher and director of teacher interns for Wayne State University; and Gwili Ford Hanna retired as an elementary school science teacher and later pursued postgraduate studies in the health sciences. Their brother, Douglas Ford Jr., earned his medical degree from Meharry Medical School and became a pediatrician. He practiced medicine in Montclair, New Jersey, for almost fifty years. The citation awarding him a Bronze Star Medal was quoted, in chapter 9 of this book, from the original document.

The children and grandchildren of these Ford siblings embraced the family's commitment to higher education and obtained undergraduate and graduate degrees from esteemed universities across the United States. Their professions include physician, attorney, educator, information technology specialist, television producer, entomologist, musician, fiction writer, newspaper editor, realtor, high school football coach, minister,

businesswoman/entrepreneur, artist, nonprofit executive, jour-
nalist, licensed master social worker, certified public accountant,
financial manager, actor, and public relations/event manager.

As for the wedding dress, all four Ford sisters wore that same
gown for their weddings. In addition, it adorned one other bride,
in 1990, at the wedding of a granddaughter of Douglas and Maber
Jackson Ford.

ABOUT THE AUTHOR

A 2017 Kresge Artist Fellow and a former attorney, Jean Alicia Elster is a professional writer of fiction for children and young adults. She is the great-granddaughter of Addie Jackson, whose family story is the basis for *How It Happens*. Elster is the author of *Who's Jim Hines?* and *The Colored Car*, which were also based on her family history and published by Wayne State University Press in 2008 and 2013, respectively; both were selected as Michigan Notable Books. Other

Photograph by Noah Stephens

awards include the Midwest Book Award in Children's Fiction, Paterson Prize Honor Book—Books for Young People, and the ArtServe Michigan's Emerging Artist Award. She is also the author of *Just Call Me Joe Joe*, *I Have a Dream, Too!*, *I'll Fly My Own Plane*, and *I'll Do the Right Thing*.